A SENSE
OF THE
WHOLE

A SENSE OF THE WHOLE

stories by

SIAMAK VOSSOUGHI

ORISON
BOOKS

Print ISBN: 978-1-949039-11-5
E-book ISBN: 978-1-949039-12-2

Orison Books
PO Box 8385
Asheville, NC 28814
www.orisonbooks.com

Distributed to the trade by Itasca Books
1-800-901-3480 / orders@itascabooks.com

Cover art: "GGP Early" (oil on board, 32" x 40"), copyright © 2011 by
John Musgrove. Used by permission of the artist.
www.musgrovepainting.com

Manufactured in the U.S.A.

ORISON
BOOKS

CONTENTS

For Molly

FOURTEEN

It was good to have a secret, the girl thought. Her mother didn't know it and her father didn't know it, and it was such a strange secret to have because it was invisible, in a way. Nothing was *outwardly* different about the world now that her brother had told her that a thing that was helping him was God. Their town was the same. It looked nice on sunny days and it looked like itself on rainy ones. She had never looked up at the sky and thought that anybody was *responsible* for the different ways it looked, and she wondered if her brother did that now. If he did, she didn't see the harm in that.

It was an exciting secret to have because she was fourteen years old and she was holding something that would turn the world upside down for her mother and her father and her aunt and uncle and everybody in the family, kids and adults. It was exciting to be trusted with that.

They still talked about him going to a therapist when they got together, and she didn't think there was anything bad about that, either. But it was the most wonderful time to hold the secret, and to look outside the window as they all talked and wonder what it was her brother saw that had God in it. Her brother was in the city and they were in their town, but whatever it was he saw didn't seem far away sometimes, because she remembered how he looked out the window at home.

In some way she didn't understand, it made sense to her that God was in the city, at least more than He was in their town. That was where everything else was, after all. It didn't mean she believed in God, but she believed in her brother believing in God. He was her brother, and they had always believed in everything about each other.

He wouldn't be doing it if it didn't help him, somehow. She knew how much he had heard all the same things as her about how God was the whole problem growing up in their house. God was the one who had wrecked their country, and who had wrecked some huge chunks of the world. God was the one who made men tell people who to be and how to live, and who did it all through fear. He was the one who had the least faith in human beings of all.

All that had nothing to do with the God her brother was talking about. He was her brother, and he hated to see all that stuff. She didn't know why it was so easy for her to know that he wasn't talking about the same God, when it would be so hard for everyone else. It would be hardest of all for her father. He and God were enemies. There was no room for generosity between them. That was the most exciting part of holding the secret, the way it was like a betrayal the size of the world.

You might know a secret about a girl and a boy in your class, but those secrets didn't fill you up like this, in a way that felt strong; like you were a full person in the world.

The person holding a secret like this one was big enough to understand about God and about no God. Which she did, somehow. She didn't *know* that she understood about them both until now. But she understood about her brother and her father. If *they* were the two sides of the God question, then she understood the God question. They just weren't opposed, that's all. Her brother and her father weren't opposed, and so God and no God weren't opposed, either. That's all there was to it.

For a secret, it could feel pretty closed up and figured out sometimes.

That was how she felt sometimes, but then other times she thought of the city and of how much it might make a person move towards God. She thought of Iran when her father was a boy and how much it might make a person move toward no God. And then the secret felt anything but closed up and figured out, because she didn't know anything about either of those places.

She looked out the window as they all talked about her brother, and she looked back at everybody and she thought they were both right, her father and her brother. They were right to be worried about him and he was right to say nobody should be worried about him. Her father would be *more* worried about him if he knew God had something to do with it. And she was still worried about him, herself. But she had seen a kind of happiness inside of his very big sadness that seemed like something he had been heading for all along. She didn't know how *much* of that had to do with God. He had told her that music sounded different to him now, that books felt different to him. Most of all, he said he couldn't afford mockery anymore. She felt happy to hear his certainty, but she felt sad because they had been real geniuses of mockery together, especially with things that deserved to be mocked.

She even remembered how they'd mocked some of the God people in their town. She guessed that was over now, but she didn't think they couldn't replace it with something.

That was the difference between her and her father. If he knew about her brother and God, there would be something irreplaceable between them.

She wondered if she would have something like that someday, something that could make her feel a betrayal the size of the world. She wondered if she would ever have an *idea* that did that. It was easy to have it with people. People did that all the time. But to have it with an idea meant that you had the idea with you all the time. It was wonderful to think about.

It was wonderful to think there was something replaceable when it came to her and her brother and God, and something irreplaceable when it came to her brother and her father, because it just meant everybody had to be who they were. It was nobody's fault. And the secret truth was, her brother and her father *could* replace it. That was the secret *inside* the secret her brother had told her. But they could do it, because God and no God still came back to love. It was crazy to see it, it was crazy to be the one to see it in a room full of older relatives. In that room, her father's silence was something to which everyone gently deferred. They waited when there was a pause for him to break it. But she knew that he didn't want to be feared. She knew that actually the *last* thing he wanted was to be feared, and so when she saw a chance, she said, "Maybe it's not that different from you, Baba."

"What do you mean?" her father said.

"You had to break away from what you knew when you were Payam's age."

She could feel her cousins looking at her with surprise that she could talk to her father like that.

"That was different. That was not the same thing at all. My family was religious. I had to leave. Look at what that religion did to our country."

She smiled. She was glad everybody could see that he didn't want to be feared. They disagreed, but they disagreed as equals, as she knew they would.

She felt like she was holding God and no God together, only she didn't feel like she was doing it by herself. She felt like the whole town and maybe even the whole world was helping her hold God and no God together. Everybody was waiting to see. Some people couldn't wait anymore, and they had to decide one way or the other. But she was fourteen years old and it could be God and it could be no God, and either way, she was glad about who she was and she was glad about who they all were and they were all trying.

"I know, Baba," she said. "But it still might not be that different. He is looking for something. You were looking for something."

Her father was quiet, and she knew he was trying to let her words have it out with something inside him. It was funny and nice how her brother trusted her with God and her father trusted her as well. She knew that if her brother kept going down the road he was going, then God and no God might have to have it out some day. But she wasn't worried about that. It was because God was along the way for her brother, along the way of the thing he wanted to do with his drawing. It would be different if God were the road and the target. It was the same with her father: No God was along the way of a better country and a better world for people.

Her aunt and her uncle and her cousins were all looking at her, but she didn't think it was anything special. It was just love, that's all. What else did they think it was all supposed to be for? Somehow, she knew inside her that the *size* of love was building toward a time

when your father and your brother would go in different directions with respect to God, and you had to try to show them that they weren't all that different at all. You had to do it without letting on about the secret your brother had told you, which was where her inner smile came from. It was like the secret had God in it. And any room where her father sat had no God in it because of a power, a force he had, a kind of courage he carried with him and imprinted on those around him, to say that he was not afraid of a world with no God. The two were true in her. Maybe it was only because she was fourteen and she hadn't come upon a point yet where she had to choose between one direction and another. In a way she hoped she never had to. She threw herself out many years ahead to a time when the world was either too empty of something beautiful, the way it was for her brother, or too full of something deceitful, the way it was for her father, so that the young woman she would be would remember there was a time when they were both true in her, that she could sit in a room that had the force of no God in it, and still hold the secret of God in her. And that she could do it easily, not like it was anything special at all, like it was a continuation of everything she had been doing that day, and even everything she had been doing all her life, or at least as long as she could remember.

THE VINE

Mr. and Mrs. Karimi came to their son's school in the evening. The school was beginning a new sexual education program, to start in sixth grade instead of seventh grade. They had invited the sixth-grade parents to come and meet the sex education teacher and ask her any questions they had.

The school was next to a swimming pool Mr. Karimi used to go to in the mornings. He had not gone since the photos of Abu Ghraib had come out. It was the locker room and being naked there. Mrs. Karimi knew that this was the reason. She could not say it. They had been married nineteen years.

There was a small part of her she felt bad about that thought, Now, you know how it is for women. Now you know how it is for our bodies. She felt bad because she thought her anger should be one hundred percent directed at the American Army for debasing the bodies of Arab men like that. And she knew what they must have done to women if they would do that to men.

"You should start going to the pool again," she said. "It is good for your back."

"I prefer walking in the evenings."

"Walking is not the same."

"I like it. I like to be outside."

"What about in the winter? It will be too cold."

"I don't mind."

When the photos had come out, it had looked to Mr. Karimi like Americans did not know what to do with their own bodies. Instead of admitting they did not know, they wanted to make somebody else look like they did not know, so it would look like they *did* know. It was very obvious to him.

At the pool, he had some American friends. He felt they would not think about why he did not come anymore.

He had felt embarrassed to have his son and daughter see the photos. He felt like they were seeing him.

Now they were going to learn about their son's sexual education at school. Okay. It must be good, Mr. Karimi thought. It must be good if it contained education.

When they arrived in the classroom, they were approached by a man whose daughter was in their son's class.

"Isn't this terrible?" the man said.

Mr. and Mrs. Karimi smiled.

"Sixth grade is too young for this," the man said.

Mr. and Mrs. Karimi smiled again. They did not know if it was terrible or not.

"Why did he come and say that to us?" Mr. Karimi said afterwards.

"He thinks that because we are Middle Eastern, we will be angry about sexual education."

Mr. Karimi laughed. "Does he think we are the Taliban?"

"I guess tonight he does," Mrs. Karimi said.

He found it funny that the man wanted them to be angry about sexual education when it was the lack of sexual education that had Mr. Karimi lost in America. It was the lack of knowing that when you make a man debase himself, you do not become a master of sex.

Mr. Karimi had not even wanted to be naked in front of his wife when he had first seen them. She had felt sorry for him then.

She would see him become quiet sometimes and she knew he was thinking of those men.

Someday, she thought, he would come out of it understanding something about women. He was not there yet. First, he had to go back to the pool.

They needed sexual education themselves, she thought. They needed a sexual education that would allow her to say to her husband, I know why you do not go back to the pool. We are just people. We can talk about these things.

But he had gone quiet out of respect for the way those men would have gone quiet. None of those men would have women they could go back to and tell.

They must know, he thought. He would look at Americans and think, they must know this was something inside themselves. Perhaps his son's sex education teacher would be able to say something about it.

She was a small, white woman, and as soon as she spoke, it was clear she had faced many men like the man who had approached them when they came in. Mrs. Karimi thought that she could be her friend. They would sit together for hours and talk about men and how much they could not say and what they could do about that. She liked the woman's pace. Not just her speaking pace, but the pace of her mind. It was pacing that made it hard for her to make friendships with American women she met. They were trying to get to everything at once, and she'd wanted to say, You'll get to everything if you get to one thing, whole.

The woman said that she came from a family who did not talk about sex. She said it was still uncomfortable to talk to her mother and father about it. That made the room soften. Mr. Karimi looked at the man who had approached them. He sat rigidly. Did the man know there was an entirely different set of circumstances under which they could have met? A set of circumstances that were the last thing Mr. Karimi saw at night when he went to sleep. He would look at the clock and he would feel thankful for time, because he imagined that time would have disappeared in that prison.

And now it was the time that the leaders in America went around saying that they would get to the bottom of it. It was a kind of show. And the people went along. And sometimes it looked to him like they wanted both: They wanted the photos and they wanted to be the ones to get to the bottom of them, too.

What was there to get to the bottom of anyway? This is how you see us, he thought. My effort is not to see anybody the way you see us.

And he knew that part of his effort should not be staying away from the pool and locker room. He knew he should go back some time.

He listened again to the sex education teacher, and he could see, too, that she was trying. She was trying to make sex into something a person would not hate in himself, and would not hate in anybody else either. He *wanted* to be able to talk to his son about sex. He had not talked to his son about the photos. He was used to talking to him about things he could have answers for.

When the teacher finished, she opened the session up to questions. The man who had approached them earlier stood up. "My daughter is eleven years old," he said. "She still plays with dolls. I don't understand how this can be the right age for talking about these things."

Mrs. Karimi felt sure as she watched him that his daughter did not play with dolls. The girl he wanted her to be played with dolls.

The teacher spoke of studies that had shown the benefits of starting the class earlier. She spoke calmly and evenly.

The man did not seem to hear. "How do we *know* we are not exposing them to something they wouldn't be thinking about otherwise? Do we *know* that?"

Mr. Karimi saw the pain on the man's face and he felt upset with himself, because now he had seen that they did not hold their pain. It came out. He wished he had not found something relatable in the man.

The teacher was quiet. She had to take her time with the question because it was only a hair's breadth away from ridiculous. She spoke even more calmly and evenly to balance him out.

Mr. Karimi knew that on the way home his wife would be angry about the man. He wanted to be angry *with* her. He did not want to feel sorry for the man. But it was the closest he had come to seeing an American man with something on his face that said, I don't know what to do with the truth of our bodies. He needed it, because in those photos of the men in Abu Ghraib, the soldiers had something on their faces that said, I know exactly what to do with the truth of our bodies. It is this. It is to relieve myself of the question.

He wondered if there was something he could say that would even things out, that would balance out his wife's anger at the man and his sorrowful ridiculousness, and he saw that it was only through the boy he had been, the boy he had felt himself to be when he had seen those photos. The photos went back to boyhood because none of them had known what bodies were and what to do with them when they were boys, and it had seemed like the soldiers wanted to take them back there again. And it had been a way to say that the work they had done to know and to understand their bodies and to even try to be good with them, didn't count. It didn't count as work, because they didn't count as men. And he simply couldn't believe that anybody who had done that work would look at it like it didn't count. And if they had something there where that work should be, then it made sense that he did not want to go to the pool and change clothes in front of his American friends, because he did not like to think about what that was.

He raised his hand to speak and as he did, he saw the man smile because he believed a Middle Eastern man would support him. In that moment, Mr. Karimi felt that the smile was the same as something that had been in those photos—something that said, I already know you, and I know you because what is inside you is static and old and has no kind of struggle resembling a vine twisting around itself and growing toward the sky. The vine in question grew along the fence in the backyard of their house. For a few years now, Mr. Karimi had looked at it as a way to remember how he was trying to be. And he knew that he had to ask his question not only *for* himself, but for the boy. The boy twisted and grew like a vine every day, and it would be too much for him if somebody were to say the boy did not have a struggle, a struggle worth respecting, because sometimes it looked for all the world to him like the vine.

The teacher saw him.

"Yes?"

"Will you teach them not to laugh at bodies?"

THE WEDDING SPEECH

"Now, there is a lot to be said about who is getting married, about the *people* who are getting married, but if you're going to be serious about this thing, you're going to have to talk about *what* is getting married, as well."

My brother was driving to pick up his suit. It was the day before his wedding to Lucy Hayes.

"A bright cold day in Seattle is marrying a bright cold day in Denver. Believe it, Sahar. That's the only way to talk about it if you're going to be serious. And I don't just mean today. Whatever I would have been doing on a day like this in Seattle when I was a boy is marrying whatever she would have been doing on a day like this in Denver when she was a girl. Do you understand the significance of that? I would've come home on a day like this and said 'what's for dinner,' and she would've come home on a day like this and eaten an apple. Those moments are marrying each other. I don't think they understand. They think it's just the *people* marrying each other."

He really loves her, I thought.

"That's just the known moments. I don't even know about all the unknown moments that are marrying each other. How are you supposed to fit all *those* into a wedding?"

"Dahlias?" I said.

"'*Dahlias?*'" my brother said. "Are you listening to what I'm saying?"

I liked hearing my brother talk about the moments marrying each other. I thought about someday marrying a boy who had an older brother who talked like that.

"They think a wedding can do that? They think a wedding can get at all the things that are marrying each other? It's insulting."

"Maybe it can get at some of them?"

"*Some?*" my brother said. "It would take a lifetime to get at them. It would take a lifetime to have any kind of a real wedding. Hold on a second."

We stopped at the tailor's and my brother went inside to get his suit.

"Another thing," he said, when he came back. "I don't know why we're limiting the guests to the people we know. If we're serious about this, we should be inviting strangers. They know a thing or two about marriage, don't they? If we're honest about it, we should have something they'll recognize, too."

"Which strangers would you invite?"

"All of them."

"'All of them?'"

"All of the ones who don't have plans tomorrow."

When I listened to him, I could almost agree with him about all the strangers who didn't have plans tomorrow coming to the wedding.

"I might have to tell them tomorrow. I might have to tell them that I appreciate their efforts, but that a real wedding requires all our lives and it requires everybody on earth. Everybody who doesn't have plans. Although, in all honesty, the decent thing for them to do would be to break their plans and make some time for it."

I felt very happy driving home and thinking about the wedding that lasted our whole lives and invited everybody on earth. So, I was surprised when I woke up in the middle of the night and suddenly felt afraid that my brother might bolt.

What if he bolted and everybody asked me if I knew anything about it and I had to say that he had said it wasn't a real wedding because people weren't making time for all the moments that were marrying each other and because we weren't inviting any strangers, but that I hadn't taken any of it seriously? Everybody would blame me, and Lucy Hayes would cry and she would try not to show that she was crying because of me, but I would still know she was. I tried to go to sleep but it was no use. I went to my brother's room. He was sleeping and I felt better. But through the night, I kept listening for a sign he might be getting out of bed to bolt. I even thought about what I would say. You're right, Dara, I would say. It isn't a real wedding because they aren't talking about all the moments that are marrying each other. You're right that it would take a lifetime to get to all of those. But don't make Lucy Hayes cry. It's not a real wedding, but marry her anyway. I started to feel sad and happy as I thought about what I would say, and I tried to stay awake to listen for him, but eventually I fell asleep.

In the morning I woke up and went to his room and he wasn't there and I thought maybe he really might have bolted, but I went to the kitchen and he was making eggs. I yawned like I hadn't been worried at all.

But the funny thing was, I felt disappointed, like I still wanted to do something with the speech I'd planned, and I guessed it was because if somebody is going to be angry at a wedding for not being the real thing because nobody is talking about all the moments that are marrying each other, then *somebody* should tell them that they're right. They're right, but that they should go to the wedding anyway.

THE HOME THING

The problem was, Mani had gotten used to a world where Iran was the home thing and America was everywhere else, the place he was part of as soon as he walked out his door, even though the boys he played with when he walked out the door were Mexican and Chinese. So, when Mrs. Pardo had said that studying history in fifth grade was going to include learning about everybody's personal histories, it had been too much for him to think of having Iran out in the open like that in the classroom, like everybody would be looking inside his house. On the day Mrs. Pardo was going to teach them about Iran, he woke up with a headache and a stomachache.

He told his mother he couldn't go to school.

He liked the idea of them learning about Iran as long as he wasn't there. He even saw himself coming to school a little proudly after they did.

His mother looked at him and said he didn't have a fever and he wasn't sneezing.

"Did those older boys take your ball again?" she said.

"No."

"Then you have to go to school," his mother said.

She didn't understand, nobody understood, and his mother and father didn't care, because nobody was going to talk about Iran at the hair salon or at his father's office, and even if they did, his mother and father didn't act different when Americans asked them about Iran. They just listened and smiled and acted like it was very natural to have a home thing and everywhere else.

And Mani felt bad when he thought it because sometimes

it *was* very natural, like when they were playing in the street and Carlos's grandfather or Dustin's mother came out and yelled in Spanish or Chinese for them to come inside. That felt good to hear.

On the school bus, he tried not to think about it. Maybe it would just be very general. Maybe she would just say that the capital of Iran is Tehran. That would be alright. That was the kind of thing anybody could find in a book. Maybe she would just stick to the facts. Every place had a lot of facts. That would be okay. He wouldn't feel so much like they were seeing inside him then.

But when he got to school, he felt even worse, because he saw his classmates, and they all looked like they'd woken up in the morning with so many other things on their mind. What if they thought that learning about Iran just got in the way of those things? What if they didn't like it? What if Nelson tried to pass a note while Mrs. Pardo was turned around? What if Jessica rolled her eyes? He didn't know what was worse—the feeling that they would all be looking inside his house, or the feeling that they would be doing that and still be bored.

He had never felt so nervous at school before. He didn't know if he could make it up the stairs. He wondered if he should just go to the front desk and tell Mrs. Kanter he was sick. She would probably be annoyed that he was sick before the school day had even begun.

He looked at all the American kids going up the stairs and he couldn't imagine how this was something they never had to worry about. They never had to worry about a home thing that was different from school and everywhere else, and it almost seemed ridiculous to him because how would you ever have anything that was secret if your home life was the same as your school life?

But it didn't help to think it was ridiculous, because he knew the American kids all thought it was perfectly natural for those two to be the same. He felt bad to think it, but he wished that Mrs. Pardo would just stick to Christopher Columbus and how many original colonies there were, because he was fine with all that stuff. He was fine with learning that stuff at school and with learning about Iran at home when he listened to his mother and father talking with the rest of his family, and anyway, they talked about Iran in Farsi, which was the way you were supposed to do it, and it brought a whole new wave of nervousness over him to think of Iran being talked about in English, because that was the school language, and he just didn't know *what* would happen if the school language and the home thing got mixed up together like that. In some distant part of himself, he felt how he'd actually worked to build the wall between home things and school things, because it just made everything clearer that way, and even though it gave him a thrill to think of not having that wall, there was something that overwhelmed the thrill, which was, he hadn't had the realization that it *was* work until just now.

He slowly walked to his classroom and Mrs. Pardo saw the way he tiredly put his books down on his desk.

"Mani," she said. "What's wrong?"

"Nothing."

The American kids were talking and laughing and remembering each other, the way they always did in the mornings, the way he usually joined in with them to do. But he didn't feel like doing it today. He looked at the board and saw that Social Studies was at its usual time, right after first recess. He didn't think he'd be able to play basketball or soccer or anything at recess today.

He didn't think about it in the morning when they had math, but at the end of math, it all came back to him again, only now it felt even worse, because he'd had a chance to see just how American his school life was. He couldn't imagine how the kids in his class could go from the way they'd been talking in the morning to something as distant as his home thing. It was too much to ask of them, he thought.

Mrs. Pardo saw his face look the way it had when he'd first come in and she asked him to stay in when the class went out to recess.

"Mani," she said. "Are you worried about Social Studies today?"

"Yes."

"Tell me what you're worried about."

"Everybody is still learning about America," he said. "Maybe they'll think it's too much to have to learn about Iran, too."

Mrs. Pardo, whose first name was Jean, had been a teacher for six years. When she listened to Mani, she remembered graduate school and a professor she'd had named Ann Ruthstein. She remembered her saying how children from immigrant families can have all sorts of reactions to having their histories integrated into the curriculum. Even *parents* from immigrant families could have all sorts of reactions to that. Ann Ruthstein said that some immigrant parents even thought that it was putting their children behind to learn about their home countries, and they should be learning about America as much as possible. Jean Pardo had felt broken-hearted to hear that. She remembered how she'd gone home and told her boyfriend about that and he hadn't shown much reaction to it one way or another, and that had been the first thing that had gotten her thinking about their eventual breakup.

"Well," she said. "Social Studies is about learning about the world. America and Iran are both part of the world."

Mani nodded. He knew America and Iran were both part of the world, but it just made everything easier if America could be the school thing and Iran could be the home thing, and he felt sad and angry that he didn't know why.

"What do you think would help you feel more comfortable?" Mrs. Pardo said.

"I want to listen," Mani said. "But I don't want anybody to see me."

"Do you want to put your chair outside the room?" Mrs. Pardo said. "I'll leave the door open."

Mani nodded.

"Okay," Mrs. Pardo said.

Mani felt better. He went outside to the schoolyard and when a ball rolled over to him from the basketball court, he picked it up and took a shot that almost went in.

After recess, Mani sat outside the classroom. Mrs. Pardo propped the door halfway open. She wondered how it would look if Mr. Willits, the principal, walked by, but she felt like she had a good explanation. She told the class Mani needed a little space.

Mrs. Pardo showed the class where Iran was on the map. Mani looked through the doorway and felt very excited. There it was, alright. How about that? His whole class was looking at it. He almost couldn't believe it.

Mrs. Pardo talked about how it used to be Persia, and she showed pictures of the ruins. Mani had never seen them before. He felt just as proud of them as if he had known about them for a long time.

Inside the classroom, Nelson raised his hand and asked to go to the bathroom.

"Hi Mani," he said.

"Hi."

"We're learning about Iran."

"I know."

"Were you born there?"

"Yes."

"Have you seen those statues?"

"No."

"Do you want to play pickle after lunch?"

"Sure."

Mani moved his chair closer to the doorway. He looked inside. They were all listening. Jessica didn't look like she was going to roll her eyes. Mrs. Pardo was talking about Iran like it was somewhere close, not far away. Mani wondered how she knew it *was* close. It was *very* close. It was even closer than *he* had realized.

"Are you in trouble, Mani?"

He turned around and saw Angela Rubey coming out of Mr. Harkness's room next door.

"No," he said.

"What are you doing out here?"

"I just felt like being outside for a while."

"Mrs. Pardo lets you do that?"

"Sometimes."

"Mr. Harkness would never let us do that."

Nelson came back from the bathroom just then.

"Kids in your class can sit outside the classroom?" Angela Rubey said.

"Only on the days that Mrs. Pardo is teaching about where you were born," said Nelson.

"I was born in Sacramento," Angela Rubey said.

"I was born here, at Children's Hospital," Nelson said.

Mani looked at them.

"I guess everybody was born somewhere," Nelson said.

He went inside the classroom and Angela Rubey got a book from her bag.

Mani looked in and saw that Mrs. Pardo was showing pictures of the *haft seen*. It sure was nice. He couldn't imagine how it must be for the kids whose home thing was always the same as the school thing. Life must be wonderful. They had this every day.

But somehow he thought that if they had this every day, they wouldn't really be seeing inside him as much as he thought. He hadn't been seeing inside them on all the other days, or if he had, it hadn't been in a rude way. Everybody's inside and outside were a lot closer than he had thought, and they were mixed up together. He had been seeing their inside by *way* of their outside. If anybody wanted to do that with him, that would be alright. Maybe he could have his inside and outside be mixed up together too.

He moved his chair to the edge of the classroom.

Mrs. Pardo read *The Little Black Fish*, a book his parents had at home. At home, his father was teaching him to read in Farsi, but Mani couldn't read it yet. Mrs. Pardo had an English version.

As the little black fish was deciding to set out to discover the end of the river, Mani picked up his chair and went back to his desk and sat down. Mrs. Pardo didn't look up or pause or anything, and he knew she wouldn't look up or pause or anything, and she knew he knew it and that was a kind of love. Everybody saw him come in and sit down, but that was alright. They *ought* to know he was nervous, because his home thing was special and important. His home thing happened to also be a world thing, but he didn't know how. He didn't remember, because it had just been a home thing for a long time now. But he *felt* how it was bigger than that, because it had a place in school, and he had always been told that school was the most important place for him to be concerned about. What all of them had—his mother and father and sister and himself—was a place in his school. He didn't know if they knew that.

THE INSULT

Amir Ali had been paid an insult. Massoud Khan, who had always seemed to have had something against Amir Ali, had, in the course of an argument at the bakery, called him the son of a whore. Its disrespectfulness was unquestionable. However, Amir Ali knew some whores. He knew three of them, in fact. And they were all pretty nice people.

Before he could reciprocate to the insult, he had to let them know it wasn't anything against them.

"It's a fine point," he explained to his younger cousin Sohrab. "If I actually were born the son of a whore, it would be difficult, but I would have to base my opinion of her on what kind of mother she was. However, Massoud Khan *meant* it as an insult."

Sohrab listened and felt very impressed by his cousin, and he thought the world certainly had some complicated dilemmas that he, too, would have to someday untangle.

Amir Ali went to the house where Fatima worked. She was standing outside. He laid it out for her.

"Yesterday Massoud Khan called me the son of a whore. This afternoon I am going to fight him. But I don't want you to think there is anything wrong with being the son of a whore."

Fatima smiled. "Then why are you going to fight him?"

"His *intention* was dishonorable."

"You are a good man, Amir Ali."

"I like to have everything in its place," he said.

From there he went to see Soraya. She actually had a son. He was a boy of five named Mohammad. When Amir Ali came to her house, he was sitting on the step in front of the house.

"Is your mother here?" Amir Ali said.

"She is sleeping," the boy said.

Amir Ali thought it wasn't the kind of thing he could pass along in a message through her son.

He picked up a rock.

"If I hit that little tree by the fence with this rock, will you give me all your pocket money?"

The boy laughed. "Yes," he said.

Amir Ali threw and missed.

"Your turn," he said.

Mohammad threw and missed.

"One step forward," Amir Ali said.

The boy took one step forward. He threw another rock and missed again.

"Two steps forward," Amir Ali said.

The boy took two steps forward and threw and missed again.

"Three steps forward."

The boy took three steps forward so that he was very close to the tree, and threw a rock and hit it. The boy smiled.

"Well done. Now, if only I had any pocket money, it would be yours."

"Can I ride your horse?"

"Yes," Amir Ali said. "When your mother wakes up, ask her permission, and I will let you ride him."

Amir Ali said goodbye and left. He had one more place to go. He went to see Ashraf Khanoom. She was officially retired. But he figured that for his purposes, it was the same thing.

She was working in her garden when he came.

"Hello, Amir Ali," she said.

"Hello."

"Look at these cucumbers."

"They are beautiful."

"Nobody knows the secret of growing good cucumbers," she said. "Including me."

"If you ever figure it out, let me know."

"I will."

Amir Ali told her about the insult and explained his reason for coming to see her.

"Massoud Khan said that?" she said.

"Yes."

"He used to come to see me, you know."

"Yes."

She pulled up a weed growing next to her cucumbers.

"I don't think you should fight him."

"I have to."

"I know Massoud Khan, and he is fighting himself," Ashraf Khanoom said. "He is fighting himself, but he doesn't know it."

"Perhaps this will help him to clarify it."

"That is what I am saying to you. It won't. It will make him think he is fighting you. It will make him feel comfortable because he will think that all this time he has been fighting you, another man. It will make him happy. I am telling you."

"What should I do then?"

"Tell him you came here. Tell him you came to see me, to tell me you did not mean anything against me in your intention to fight him."

"I did not come only to see you. I went to see Fatima and Soraya."

"Tell him that, too," she said. "How are they?"

"Fatima is well and Soraya was asleep."

"Alright. Well, tell him. He would come to see me and I could see he had been fighting himself. The important thing was, the way a man would leave. The ones who would leave as though they were a different man from how they had come in, I felt sorry for. When I was younger, I liked them because it used to make me feel good that I could change them from one man to another. But after a while, I felt sorry for them. When they left and they looked like they thought the fight in themselves was over, I felt very sorry for them."

Amir Ali felt himself losing track of just whose honor he would be defending in fighting Massoud Khan--his own, or Ashraf Khanoom's, or that of whores everywhere. He would have to give it some more thought. And he would have to tell Sohrab that the matter was even more complicated than he had thought.

But standing there with Ashraf Khanoom in her garden, he did feel less compelled to fight Massoud Khan. He felt it was important to listen to what she said, at least as important as it was for Sohrab to listen to him.

"You give me hope, Amir Ali," Ashraf Khanoom said.

"Me?"

"Yes."

The cucumbers smelled very fresh and clean. They *were* beautiful, Amir Ali thought. He wished he could stand there in their smell all day.

"I know one thing about growing good cucumbers," he said.

"What is that?"

"Start here. Start in Iran."

Ashraf Khanoom laughed. "Well, I can do that, at least."

SHARPNESS

The thing about a man with a gun is that now he has aims, now he has something he's pointed at, which makes him sharp. Now he's more than just a ball rolling around bouncing off other balls. So it makes sense that when writers have sat down to write, they've often worked with a man who has a gun. It makes sense that they've needed him to be sharp. His sharpness is often the thing that lets them find the story.

I wanted to write about a man who was just as sharp without guns, but I didn't know how. I had just come to San Francisco and I was working at a school as a playground monitor. Every recess was fascinating because I could just watch people and see who they were. One thing I saw was that boys wanted to be sharp just as much as men. I could sometimes feel just as lonely among them in my looking for a new way to be sharp, myself. But not for very long, because they were kids, so they were wonderful.

Among the teachers of the third-grade boys, there were two schools of thought when it came to their playing gun games. The boys in Mrs. Hampton's class were not allowed to play gun games and the boys in Mr. Verdi's class were. This did not make the boys in Mr. Verdi's class go after the boys in Mrs. Hampton's class. There was no fun in shooting somebody who couldn't play. But sometimes I would see the boys in Mrs. Hampton's class watching the boys in Mr. Verdi's class, watching the sharpness with which they could duck around a corner and turn and fire one last shot. The way they could close one eye and aim their finger at someone across the play structure. The boys in Mrs. Hampton's class would look a little hopeless, like they were never going to know what it was to feel as clean and pointed as a gun, like they were going to stay unsure and shapeless forever.

I was glad to see it, because I always felt hopeful to see that boys and men were in the same struggle together. It was better than thinking there was a clear dividing line between them. That was there too, but it didn't tell the whole story.

My first attempt at getting the boys in Mrs. Hampton's class to do something other than watch the boys in Mr. Verdi's class was touch football. There was something very clean and pointed to a ball being thrown just past a defender's hands and being caught for a touchdown pass. But there were kids who could play, and kids who couldn't. They didn't say it, but they knew there was something egalitarian about gun games. Anybody had a chance of shooting anybody. The football games turned into two-on-two, and then pretty soon, that petered out as well.

One day I was sitting on the bench next to Devon, who was in Mrs. Hampton's class.

"I wish we could play shooting games," he said.

"Mrs. Hampton has that rule for a reason," I said.

"What is the reason?"

"You should ask her."

At home in the evenings, I was writing different stories, trying to find the man who was just as sharp without guns. At first, I thought he drew his sharpness from how distant he felt from the world, but I wasn't so sure. There was a man I would see walking home who stood, asking for change, and he would smile at me beautifully when I gave him a quarter. His smile was closer to what

I was looking for.

Where I lived, there were boys with guns. I knew, because one had pointed his at me. For two or three days afterwards, it had been difficult to watch the boys in Mr. Verdi's class playing with their fingers for guns, and then it felt like it had before. But I agreed with Mrs. Hampton's rule. There was something about boys playing gun games in a world where boys had guns. It did not seem right.

A couple days after we talked, Devon told me he'd talked with Mrs. Hampton about the rule.

"What was her reason?" I said.

"Well, I didn't actually ask her why she has the rule."

"What did you ask her?"

"I asked her if instead of shooting bullets, we could shoot lasers from our guns. She said no. Then I asked her if we could just shoot whipped cream from them."

"Whipped cream?"

"Yes. Then the person we shot at would just get whipped cream all over them."

"What did she say?"

"She said no."

"Why didn't you ask her the reason for the rule?"

He looked off to the side. "Because I know it's a good rule. I just don't think it's fair that the boys in Mr. Verdi's class get to play those games and we don't."

"I understand that. You think it should be the same rule for everybody."

"Yes."

"Did you tell Mrs. Hampton that?"

"No, because if she talks to Mr. Verdi about it, and he tells the boys in his class that they can't play it any more, they might get mad at me."

"Okay," I said. "I'll talk to her about it."

At the end of the day I told Mrs. Hampton about it and she agreed that the rule ought to be consistent. On the way home, I thought about the boys in Mr. Verdi's class. They were going to have to find something new. Well, it would be a good practice for them for finding who they were without guns. If any of them grew up to be writers who wanted to write like that, they'd have had a little experience.

If a man wanted to write like that, he couldn't be halfway about it. That's what I was learning in those days. I couldn't go home and watch a television program in which the characters expressed their sharpness through gunfire. I had nothing against those programs or those characters, I just felt further away from understanding what guns really were when I watched them. I felt further away from knowing how to write without them. And I realized the key to watching those programs was identifying with the shooter. But there was nothing to stop me from identifying with the man who got shot. They usually accounted for this by making the man who got shot a villain. But there was no getting around the fact that the man who got shot had once been a boy.

I had a friend or two tell me I was overthinking it, but when I walked home and saw the smile of the man asking for change and the corner where the boy had pointed a gun at me, I didn't think I was.

There was no getting around the fact that writers had to know who they were in relation to guns. They had to pick them up or not pick them up, but if they were going to not pick them up, they had to *all the way* not pick them up. They had to not pick them up with the same decisiveness as men who picked them up.

By the end of the week the boys in Mr. Verdi's class were not allowed to play gun games anymore. They moved around lazily and uncertainly in the schoolyard, but it opened up a world to the boys in Mrs. Hampton's class. They didn't have to sit and watch to see the sharpness they wanted to see enacted anymore. They had running races and they played handball and four-square, and they even organized games of football for themselves. It was good to see, and I knew the boys in Mr. Verdi's class would come around. They didn't have anybody they could watch and see possessing that special thing just by a move with their fingers. There was only the slow way.

The boy who had pointed a gun at me didn't have a chance for the slow way, didn't have as much of a chance as the boys I knew, at least. When I tried to hate him, there were so many feelings that came before hate, that hating him would get lost. Hating him was a gun, and all the other feelings were all the other games that I watched the boys in Mrs. Hampton's class play. That was how I'd thought about it the next day, how I'd almost lost the chance of ever watching those kids play again.

I'll take the slow way, I thought. I'll take the slow way with writing and watching over kids and everything. I'll take the slow way, because the slow way lets you see how much is right in front of you, and I wouldn't trade that for any kind of fast way. I was learning from the playground how much was right in front of me, and I felt like if I could do that in writing, I'd be in business.

The boys in Mrs. Hampton's class brought the boys in Mr. Verdi's class into their games, and pretty soon I was sitting on the bench by myself, which was fine. It was easy to think when a man sat down to write, that his best subject matter were men who had been decisive in picking up a gun, but I didn't believe it. His best subject matter was life, and it took whatever form it took in front of him. If he was lucky enough to see it take the form of boys playing, it didn't do anybody any good to say that was less important than men and guns.

Just before the bell rang, Devon walked up to me and asked me to spin a basketball on my finger and then slide it to his finger, his way of saying thanks for me talking with Mrs. Hampton.

"You know I didn't want to do the shooting games because I wanted to kill anybody, right?" he said.

"Sure," I said. "Why did you want to do it?"

"It just looked fun. It looked fun to run and hide behind something and aim."

"I understand."

"It wasn't because I wanted to hurt anybody."

"Yes. I remember you said you thought it was a good rule."

He smiled to see his own consistency.

"Why do you think it's a good rule?"

"Well, guns are bad, I know that. But there's something you can be with them that you can't be the rest of the time."

"I'm hoping to find a way to be that, the rest of the time."

"How are you going to do that?"

"I don't know," I said. "Love?"

He looked at me. "That might work."

"It's worth a try, don't you think?"

He nodded. "That really might work, Paymon."

It was breathtaking to see in his face that those were the two options before me. It was better than any television program.

THE TUNE

Kamran Mohammadizadeh was sitting at home when his phone rang.

"Kamran! This is Sophia. I know you might think this is crazy, but I'm in Chicago and my cab driver is Iranian. I got excited. He's nice the same way you're nice."

Americans are a cute people, Kamran thought. That was the best way to look at it. The thing about Sophia though was that if she was calling like this, it really was because the cab driver was nice the same way he was nice.

"Do you want to talk to him?"

"Sure."

She put the cab driver on the phone.

"Hello, sir."

"Hello, sir."

"These American women," Kamran said.

The cab driver laughed. Kamran could imagine Sophia's face, happy that they were already getting along so well.

"What can you do?" the cab driver said. "An American woman gets in my cab and says, 'You're Iranian? I know a man in San Francisco who is Iranian.' What can you do?"

"Nothing," Kamran said.

"She was very happy to talk about you."

"That is nice."

The cab driver was quiet, as an Iranian way of saying: I will not pry, but she is a friendly and attractive woman, and I can see that you are in San Francisco while she is here in Chicago, but the way she spoke up excitedly about you was no small thing, and of course I won't pry—the nature of your relationship is of course between you and her—but to whatever degree you want to continue your relationship with her, despite your separation, I am for it. I am a man who has known ups and downs in my own life, both here in America and in Iran, and I believe I can recognize a woman worth knowing when I see one, and I just want you to know, as one countryman to another, that if I were you, I would not let the distance between you close off whatever relationship you may have.

"That is nice," Kamran said again, as an Iranian way of saying: Thanks.

"How long have you driven a cab?" Kamran said.

"Five years. Two years in New York, three years in Chicago."

"How long did it take you to learn the streets of Chicago?"

"One year. How long have you known this woman?"

"One year. I don't know her as well as you know the streets of Chicago, though."

The cab driver laughed.

"I do not believe you," he said. "The way she talked about you, you must know her well."

"No," Kamran said. "She won't tell me what happened in her past to make her this way."

"What way?"

"This way that she likes me the most when she is far away. If she were to go as far away as some place like Iran, she would love me. In Chicago, she likes me a lot."

"Ah. I would take her to Iran for you if I could."

"Thank you. She would be calling me all the time if she went there. There are a lot of Iranians there."

"Yes, there are."

"Do you think all interesting women have to be crazy?"

"I do not think this is the right question."

"I know. I'm sorry."

"Let me ask you—if she did tell you what happened in her past to make her like this, do you think it would help?"

"Yes. It would help because if she talks about it, maybe it would be the start of changing it."

"Maybe. But if she told you and it did not change anything, that could be worse."

"Why?"

"Because you would know. It is often better to not know. In my own life, there is a lot that I don't know. I don't know why I am in Chicago driving a taxi. But I know these streets. I know what I can know."

Kamran was quiet. He had not tried knowing only what he could know with Sophia Penn for a long time. Knowing what he could know with her meant talking only about today. She could talk forever about today, almost like they had no pasts when they were together. Although, she would listen to his past. But half a past didn't cut it. When only one person's past was laid out on the table, it felt like storytelling, like something there for entertainment.

Maybe it made him sadder because he himself would be nothing without his past, without an Iran he had left as a little boy, without the ability to talk at length with an Iranian cab driver in Chicago at the drop of a hat. Still, it helped that she was the subject matter.

"Is she going to live in Chicago?" the cab driver said.

"No, she is there to perform in a play."

"Are you going to come to see it?"

"I don't know."

"If you came, you could stay at my house. I will give you my number."

"Thank you. What has she been doing all this time we have been talking?"

"She is smiling. She looks very happy."

"Hello," the cab driver said to Sophia.

"Hello," she said. "Your language is very beautiful."

"Did you hear that?"

"Yes," Kamran said. "Our language is very beautiful." He felt sad about how beautiful their language was. It was something having to do with the limitations of words. He felt too tired to go into it much and told himself he'd think about it later.

He felt angry, too, because Americans always said that Farsi sounded beautiful, but with Sophia, he knew she meant it. She could just dance over the whole thing, his whole past and his effort to be in America as a force of resistance and at the same time as someone with his own soft dreams about Chicago.

If he were inclined to think like this, he would think her game all along was for her to know him better than he knew her. There were times when she would ask him something and when he answered, at the end of it he would say, "What about you?"

"No," she would say.

"No what?"

"No, because I have something else to ask you."

All over the world, he would think, people wished the other person would listen as much as they spoke. He was a man who was wishing a woman would speak as much as she listened.

It's a good thing I'm not inclined to think that way, he thought

The cab driver was right. It was better to not know. He could just be sad as long as he didn't know, and sadness was a thing he knew. He knew how to hold that, walking down the street. He knew where it lived in his body.

"Well," the cab driver said. "It was good to talk to you, sir."

"It was good to talk to you, sir."

"Any time you are in Chicago..."

"Thank you. Any time you are in San Francisco..."

The driver laughed. It was an adventure to be Iranians in their own American cities, but it was an adventure to be alive, so all they were was right.

"I'll let you talk with her."

"Thank you."

"See?" she said.

"Yes," Kamran said.

"I knew you would like him."

"You were right."

"I wouldn't have called for any Iranian, you know."

"I know."

"As soon as we started talking, I knew it. What did you talk about?"

"Just life."

She laughed. "I knew it. I knew you would talk about life."

"Yes."

THE TUNE

See how easy it is, he felt like saying. See how easy it is for two people to talk about life when they know they're not going to do anything bad with anything they say. They're not going to take what they say and hold it somewhere secretive and dark. They're going to let it be just as open as it was when it was inside one person, free to fly around in there however it wanted, that's all.

But he would be knowing if he said that. He had to give not knowing a shot. He had to move with the uncertainty of why he was in San Francisco, why the cab driver was in Chicago, why she was happiest when she could give the phone to two other people and let them talk. It was very funny. It was musical too, though not with a tune he could hear just yet. Just because he couldn't hear it yet didn't mean it wasn't there.

BREAD

Charlie Vartridge was a socialist. His neighbor, Darryl Shrews, was not. Here are the things that kept them friends: Raking leaves, time, wives who had left them and new wives they had married.

They had gotten to where they could argue freely, because they had lived life next door to each other and they had seen the troubles it had, which they both unspokenly admitted it might have under any economic system.

"You take that new bakery that opened up on Madison," Charlie said one day in spring.

"Alright, what of it?" Darryl said.

It was a continuous conversation. The subject was the same. What kind of world should it be?

"I went in there and smelled the bread baking last week. And I thought, this place is more than just a place for me to buy bread."

Darryl looked at his friend. They both had a deep and abiding love for work. He thought he knew where this was going.

"That smell," Charlie said. "I was so proud of them. I was so proud of the men and women who were responsible for that smell. I could tell that they cared. I could tell they cared enough about me for the smell to hit me like that. They're the ones, the people working away in the kitchen. They are the story of bread."

"Still needed somebody to buy all that equipment, didn't they?" Darryl said. "Still needed somebody to buy all those ingredients."

"Money," Charlie said. "Alright, so he's got money. I'm not talking about money. I'm talking about bread. Who makes that smell? That's who makes the bread. That's who the place belongs to."

"I used to go to Mike Summers's bakery on Richmond. He owned the place," Darryl said. "He'd say hello to everybody. I'd want to buy bread even if I didn't need it just to say hi to him." ·

Charlie looked at his friend. "I'm not saying there can't be friendliness under capitalism. But there's a brotherhood of men that's beyond friendliness. It's just logical. How come you have a rake and I have a rake? How come we don't have a community rake that you use on Mondays and I use on Tuesdays? It's just logic."

"Because I might want to rake on Tuesday."

"You wouldn't need to if you'd raked on Monday."

"I might want to do something else on Monday."

"But you'd have a responsibility to your neighbors to do it on your day. And they'd have a responsibility to do it on theirs. What's wrong with that?"

"I've got a responsibility to my family. I've got a responsibility to them to keep the yard clear of leaves."

The conversation had started before their wives had left them, but it had only really gotten going afterwards. They had spoken in hints and subtleties before then, but they had no secrets now, at least not ideological ones.

They knew the conversation they had was an uncommon one. They knew it usually came with all kinds of bluster behind it, but it felt good to have nothing behind it but two men saying goodbye at the end of it and walking back to their own garages.

"Alright, you take Mike Summers's bakery. Now, I don't know why it went under, but it might have had to do with that Lucky's that opened up around the corner. That happens. Now, why should he have to go out of business over that?"

"The big fish eat the small fish," Darryl said.

Charlie smiled. "There are a lot more small fish than there are big fish."

"So?"

"So, the small fish can say, we've had it with this. We're going to do something different."

"Eventually, somebody will want to be a big fish again," Darryl said.

Eventually somebody will want to have something more. It hung over their conversation like a ghost. Eventually somebody will want to have something more and it'll be somebody you thought you knew well and there won't be anything you can do.

Charlie laughed, to shake them both out of it. "Alright, but what about you? Do you want to be a big fish? Or would you rather everybody had enough that they could survive and have a decent life?"

"It doesn't matter what I want," Darryl said.

"Doesn't matter?" Charlie laughed. "Of course, it matters!"

"It's going to be what it's going to be."

"But you could say that about a lot of things."

"I do."

Charlie's wife left him for a woman and Darryl's wife left him for spiritual enlightenment. She might be with a woman now, too, for all he knew. Both men had like-minded friends whom they had not told anything about their conversations. They had come close, when their friends would joke about people with the other's point of view. But there was something about the conversation that made them want to keep it their own thing.

"History would suggest it isn't just going to be what it's going to be," Charlie said. "It would suggest there are all kinds of decisions that people make that determine what it's going to be."

"Who makes those decisions?" Darryl said. "The guys on top."

"Not always. Not even most of the time."

It had been a tough road, but Charlie had decided he wasn't going to hold his wife's leaving him against the people. He had decided he wasn't going to hold it against women and he wasn't even going to hold it against women who leave their husbands for other women. He hadn't ever guessed that Karl Marx would help him to not do all that, but he had.

It was something connected to the smell of the bakery, and why he wanted his friend to know what he meant about the place: If the smell of the bread was connected to the work, then he could take pride in the work, and then he could take pride in his own work, which included making peace with the past. He didn't know what kind of peace Darryl had found. He knew that he went to his job every day and took care of his kids and raked the leaves in his yard. But there were moments when Charlie genuinely felt like a participant in his own history, not just the object of it, by the choices he made. It was a choice to associate the smell of the bread with an appreciation for the baker, before that of his own stomach. He wanted Darryl to know these things because he thought it would help him.

"I don't know what world you're living in," Darryl said. "But that's not how it looks to me. All I see is the people at the top control the strings."

"Sure," Charlie said. "But there's so much that they don't control, too."

This is what it always came back to: belief. Charlie wanted to be careful because whatever belief or non-belief his friend had, he'd had enough of something inside himself to have gotten this far, to have survived something Charlie had survived himself, and there was no rule that said two men had to survive something in the same way. He wanted to say what he had to say in a way that said, this is still the important thing—the two of us talking, remembering ourselves, trying to be something in conversation as good as the bread in its baking.

"They don't control this," Charlie said. "Us talking together."

Darryl looked off into the distance. "Where's it gotten us, though?"

"To today," Charlie said. "Maybe even a little bit of tomorrow."

"Yes," Darryl said. "That's true."

"We'll go to the bakery on Madison some time," Charlie said. "You'll see what I mean. You'll smell the bread and you'll know what I mean."

It was all talk. They had never gone anywhere together. Their friendship was confined to the sidewalk between their houses.

"You think I'm going to come out of there thinking like you?" Darryl said. "That's going to take some pretty powerful bread."

Charlie laughed. "It is," he said.

It was, too. He believed that if they ever went to the bakery together, the smell would convince Darryl the only thing that mattered about a bakery was the bread and the people making it. He believed it already. It was just that his belief came out in the memory of individuals like Mike Summers, instead of the world.

They had a good thing going, though, coming at it from different points of view. Charlie couldn't imagine how it would be if they had been agreeing all this time. He had a couple of friends at the university for that. But it was good to see that their troubles ran through the political spectrum, through history and the interpretations thereof. He knew they would keep talking. He knew they were never going to agree, and he felt glad about that.

THE OVERPAYMENT

Down at the store they overpaid me by six hours. They wrote that I'd worked twenty-six hours and I'd only worked twenty that week. So, I went down there on my day off to see Tony and lose some money.

Tony was sitting at his desk.

"That's the nicest thing I've ever seen," Tony said.

I thought he was going to cry.

"You know I never would've noticed this?" he said.

"Well, there it is," I said.

"You're a good kid, Ray."

"Forget it."

"My son, he's mixed up in drugs now," Tony said. "It's no use pretending about it. I don't even know where he is. You should see his mother. A wreck."

I almost felt like I shouldn't have said anything, he looked so miserable.

"But you're a good guy, Ray."

"Never mind good," I said. "If I tried to get away with it, next thing you know I'll tell some girl I don't love that I love her. Then I'll get married and lose some real money. I'm just being practical."

He laughed.

"I wish my son was practical like you."

"He might be," I said. "I know some guys who've disappeared like that. He'll be alright."

"Do you know what I do at night?" he said. "I drive up and down Haight Street looking for him."

I felt mad at the world when he said that. For making a guy like

Tony's son think disappearing was the practical thing to do.

"He'll be back," I said.

"I see what you mean about the money," Tony said. "And telling a girl you don't love that you love her. I hope you can tell some girl that you *do* love that you love her."

"Thanks Tony," I said. "I'll start with all the girls who want to meet a guy who works part-time and draws comics."

"Don't worry," he said. "You'll find somebody."

I just wanted to make him laugh. The truth was there was a girl I was going to meet tonight. I didn't think I was going to love her.

"I don't know about this one, Ray," he said. "Everything else I've known what to do. With this one I just want to grab him and love him, but that's not enough. That's not going to do it."

"Yes," I said.

What was going to do it? A different world? It might take less than that for Tony's son, but there were going to be other mothers and fathers driving up and down Haight Street looking for their kids. It was a fine line for everybody. That was why I was scared of a thing like not telling Tony about being overpaid in the first place.

It was because back when I was close to disappearing, when my father had wanted to just grab me and love me even though he knew that wasn't enough, I had decided to admit to myself how scared I was, how scared I was that what was inside every man was inside me, that I was always going to be a mystery to myself, and all I could do were small things to figure that out a little.

I wasn't lying when I told him it was a matter of practicality.

"I'm going to finish up here and head home," Tony said. "And then I'll head out there again tonight."

"Listen," I said. "I'll go out there with you tonight."

"You don't have to do that."

"It'll be good to have two people. We can each look on one side of the street."

My father had never had to drive around looking for me. But it was close. He'd always known where I was, but he'd been just about as worried about me as Tony was now. He'd come down from Seattle and I'd hated to see him worried like that, but I'd had to be honest that I couldn't look in any direction and not see death, except when I sat down to draw at my desk.

"Alright," he'd said. "Then sit down and draw for as long as you need to."

It was the best thing anybody could've said to me.

Now I had to do everything I could to have something worth drawing when I sat there.

"What time are you going?" I said.

"Eight o'clock."

"Okay. Come by my place on the way."

"Okay, Ray."

I went home to call the girl I was supposed to meet and tell her. I figured I'd tell her the truth. I'd see if she could meet me tomorrow night. If she asked me how come I didn't look for Tony's son with him tomorrow night, I'd tell her I had to do what I could to make him feel like we would find him tonight. I figured she could see the practicality of that.

YOU ARE MY BROTHER

There was talk in the paper again, another war in the Middle East, and the men in the store knew only that here in Rafferty's News and Sundries, they would not have to do what they would have to do outside the store, which was to act like it was very far away or even like it was not happening. It was a place to talk. Old Man Rafferty had made it that way. Too many people took in the news by themselves in America, he believed. He'd wanted a place like the kind he remembered from Ireland, where the news was not only received, but discussed. If things got heated, that was where the skill of the man running the store came into play. It was not unlike a bartender's skill. If men cared about the world around them, they could find the fighting parts of themselves from the news faster than they could from alcohol. Now, a bartender could always tell them to step outside. Old Man Rafferty had only had to do that once in twenty-eight years. His talent lay in making sure it stayed in the realm of words, and ensuring that an argument was valued according to rhetorical merit. All this was something he tried to explain to his nephew, Tom Pence, when Rafferty cut back to just weekends and let Tom take over the rest of the days. Tom thought about his uncle's words that morning when he saw the headline in the paper.

The men still expected to talk. Tom had already seen that it didn't depend on his uncle's presence, which was part of the place now. He'd realized that working there made *him* care more than he had before. The best way to keep things peaceful was to make people feel heard. And they could tell if that was faked. It didn't mean that he had to agree. The customers who spoke up wanted to know how he really felt. They wanted a back-and-forth. He wondered if it might be the only chance for it they had in a day.

There was a man who came in who was Arab. Tom did not know his name. He was happy to talk to Tom about sports, but he got quiet when the talk turned to politics. It was not the quiet of having nothing to say. It wasn't the quiet of buying what he needed and leaving the store, either. It was the quiet of a sad curiosity. He looked like there was something he was trying to understand.

The morning of the war headline, the Arab was at the counter when Durell, who came in every morning, called out, "Now I have to worry about my cousin. He might get sent over there. He's in Germany."

The Arab looked at him. Now this is a thing, Tom thought. An Arab man and a black man and the U.S. Army and war.

"You are my brother," the Arab said. "But I don't want your cousin to go and I don't want anybody to go."

"You are *my* brother," Durell said. "But that is my cousin. If he goes, then I have to support him when he is there."

"You are still my brother," the Arab said. "But there are people there who are going to be killed in this war. I am not talking about your cousin now. I do not know him. I respect that he is your cousin. But I do not respect war."

"You are still *my* brother," Durell said. "But I am going to pray for my cousin if he goes there. I have to."

Tom Pence stood silently and watched. He did not know if the men were arguing or not. Their words were not arguing, but there was a fire there. He saw that it wasn't a new fire. It had been there the whole time he had known both men, and before that as well. His uncle had a fire like that, and his uncle's Irish friends.

The Arab paid for his items and did not leave. There was nothing aggressive in the way he did not leave. Durell brought his coffee to the counter to pay for it and there was nothing aggressive in the way he did it, either. This was familiar for them, Tom Pence realized. There was nothing aggressive in it because it was not new. It was a slightly more overt expression of how they moved through the world.

They stood face to face now.

"You're my brother," the Arab said. "But those are my people."

"You're my brother, too," Durell said. "But that's my cousin."

The Arab sighed. "So, if it were just me and you then, I guess there would be no war."

"Yes," Durell said. "If it were just me and you, there would be no war. We would just come in here to Rafferty's and drink this bad coffee." He smiled at Tom.

"Ha ha," the Arab said. "Yes, it is terrible coffee."

Durell extended his hand. "It *is* terrible coffee."

The Arab shook it. His face looked sad. "It is very bad."

Tom Pence did not feel insulted about the coffee. He felt proud to have it be a part of their peace process.

"I hope your cousin comes out of it okay," the Arab said.

"I hope your people come out of it okay," Durell said.

The Arab smiled and walked out. Durell put the coffee on the counter and paid for it. As he was leaving, Tom Pence wanted to call out to him to wait. He wanted to ask him if what had just happened was an ordinary thing. He wanted to ask if it was the kind of thing a guy did in the morning and then went about his day. Because to him, it had looked miraculous.

"Do you know him?" he asked Durell.

"Him? No," Durell said. "I've seen him around."

When his uncle came in to check on things in the afternoon, Tom told him about what had happened in the morning. Old Man Rafferty smiled.

"I didn't know what to do," Tom said.

"Sounds like you didn't need to do anything," his uncle said.

"But if I don't do anything, then . . . "

Old Man Rafferty smiled interestedly. "Then, what?"

Tom Pence wondered himself: Yes, then what? He felt too embarrassed to go on.

Old Man Rafferty laughed. "This is the American in you talking, boy. You're a conductor, you're not a warden. You've got to let the people talk. In America, they say that if everybody stays good and silent, then you've got peace." He picked up the paper. "War! What the hell do they think, people are going to stay silent about a thing like that? That people are going to see a headline like that and not let their hearts come out? I don't understand this place. I've been here forty-four years but I don't understand it."

Tom Pence didn't understand it, either. He'd been happy to see Durell and the Arab talking this morning. He'd even wanted to ask if it was a miracle. But somehow, when he told the story, he put himself in the position of some kind of arbiter, some kind of last word on the matter, when in fact he hadn't had a single word to say. The newspaper said war, so he guessed there had to be a war. His uncle was right—he hadn't needed to do anything. So, what was he in relation to war, in relation to the two men? He couldn't be under them, he couldn't be looking up at the realm of their discourse. Why not? he thought. Because the headline, the headline *was* his voice. It said war, so that meant war. This thing Durell and the Arab had, this thing his uncle had, he did not have it. How was he supposed to get it? He was thirty-years-old, so he'd not had it for a long time.

And then, because he *was* American, he asked himself what value it really had. What value did it really have in the face of a thing like war? Of the three things that had been at work in the morning, the Arab, Durell, and war, what had been the biggest? War. So, what had been the truest? What was the side to be on in the long run? It was the side of the headline.

"Well," he said to his uncle. "It's not like it's going to change anything."

His uncle looked crestfallen.

"You know better than to say a thing like that."

Tom Pence felt ashamed because he did know better, but he'd gone down a path he had to stay on.

"The paper says war, that means there's a war," he said. He was sickened and disgusted with himself, but it came out like he was sickened and disgusted with his uncle's belief in having a place for people to talk.

Old Man Rafferty went to the back of the store, touching and straightening a few things along the way. Tom Pence stood at the counter. A woman bought a magazine and cigarettes. A boy looked at a car magazine and left.

Tom knew that technically he was correct. If the paper said war, that meant war. But he also knew the thing that happened in the morning was the kind of thing his uncle had always hoped his store would be the setting for. It was the kind of thing *he* hoped the store could be the setting for, too. But something had gotten lost in the telling. How was he supposed to think of the paper if two men could rise above it as easily as that? How was he supposed to think of a voice that was his voice? He'd told his uncle like it was a nice little story for when a man was down on the ground, away from and underneath the serious business of war. Why had he told it to him like that?

He was American, and everybody wanted to come here, didn't they? Everybody wanted to come here and be part of America, didn't they? Men like his uncle, and his uncle's friends. How was he supposed to look *up* at them? How was he supposed to *stay* looking up at them? Where was he supposed to do that from? That was no place. No place he knew, at least. It was no place he saw in the newspapers or magazines. You didn't look up at the world because ultimately, you were where everybody was trying to be. A thing like what he had seen this morning—it was nice and it was beautiful, but it wasn't the cold, hard world of the newspaper headline, and what he felt like he understood that nobody else understood, not the Arab or Durell or his uncle, was that you had to call it a cold, hard world before you could get somewhere in it. And it was true he was working at his uncle's store, just like his uncle had done, but he sure wasn't going to be doing that for twenty-eight years. He sure was going to get somewhere else.

That thing he'd seen them do this morning, that thing with calling each other "my brother," where were they *really* going to take that, anyway? Where were they really going to go with it? Tom Pence didn't know where his own life was going to go, but he felt like his best chance was on the side of the headline, even when the headline said war. *War* was going somewhere at least. He felt ashamed to think it, but he just wanted *something* to be going somewhere, all this time that he stood behind the counter at Rafferty's and a big, unreachable world was happening in the newspaper, and even the people who came in and bought a lousy pack of gum looked like they had every opportunity for adventure and drama and life when they left the store.

His uncle came back from the storeroom.

"Do you really think that thing this morning doesn't change anything?" Old Man Rafferty said.

Tom Pence looked down.

"It changed me, you know," his uncle said. "It changed me and I wasn't even there."

Me too, Tom Pence wanted to say. It changed me, too. But I don't know to *what*, and I know that has to do with something I don't know to begin with, but I don't even know what *that* is, and it's just a whole lot easier to just go with the headline, to just go with what the headline says. If there's a war, then there's a war. I know this is a place where people expect to talk, but I don't know what the change is when they talk like that, when I'm still here behind the counter and the people come and go, and when nobody can tell me—change to *what*?

FAME

They were just such stars, that's all. He thought of Gabriel Adler, in his house at night, knowing that tomorrow he would come to a place where the other kids would see him and think, there's Gabriel, and it would be nothing but an addition, and Gabriel would know it was nothing but an addition, easily and effortlessly, not like it was anything special at all, and they would all just jump into being eleven-year-old boys and girls together, which itself wasn't *easy*, but it was . . . whatever the word was for when you were allowed to be *all* of eleven. He hadn't known how much space it took to be all of eleven, but it only took a few months of working at the small progressive-education, private school to know he hadn't had it as a kid in public school back home.

It wasn't a complaint, it was just a wonder. You could come to school and you could know that the things on your mind and in your heart had a reasonable amount of a home there. If you were a boy, you could know that you *had* a heart, and that it was a worthwhile thing. It didn't have to come as a surprise later on. That alone changed the world, he thought. Who would I have been if I'd gone to a school like that, he thought for the millionth time. He had already seen boys go from the greatest hardness inside themselves to the greatest softness. That could have been all of us, he thought. But they'd had a much smaller space to work with. They *could've* all been just as big, though.

And it wasn't just a matter of the boys and who they could be. There was Gabriel Adler and the way he walked into the classroom, but there was also Rebecca Maury and Mina Powell and the way that shy and quiet girls were still stars, too, because being shy and quiet was part of the story of being eleven, too. And it wasn't just eleven, either. There was stardom in all the kids there, a very casual stardom none of the kids knew they had. Maybe all that school did was try not to put it out. Of course, somebody might say that the world was going to put it out, so you might as well get used to that at school. That was more like the schooling he'd had and remembered. But you could just as easily say the world wouldn't put it out, if a kid got used to not having it put out. Who knew? The thing that stuck with him though, was that children naturally gravitated toward stardom—toward *some* kind of stardom—when there wasn't something around them that *set out* to put it out.

These were the thoughts he had while Alice Peru was in the shower. This was his third time in her bed. It was nice to lie in her bed and think about the kids at the school. There was a part of him that was thinking about them all the time, but it was the difference between his thoughts of them being a river he was sailing down versus sitting on a bank watching it go by.

When she came back, she said, "What were you thinking about?"

"I was thinking about how famous we were as kids."

"Who?"

"All of us."

This was why Alice Peru liked having him in her bed.

"It may be that we were famous because we didn't know how famous we were. In which case, I suppose there is something paradoxical about fame."

"Were *you* famous?"

"Yes. I had some famous moments. Although I don't remember them very well. But I do remember that the world started telling me pretty early that I wasn't famous."

"How did it do that?"

"By telling me that my *main* job was to go from first grade to second grade. And from second grade to third grade. Like that. I know I had to do that, but that wasn't really my *main* job."

"What was your main job?"

"My main job was to be a person."

She got into bed with him.

"I am still learning how to do that," Alice Peru said.

"Me too. I just wish somebody had told me it was my main job. I didn't really know it until I saw that it was a kid's main job. The funny thing is, when you tell a kid that's their main job, they say, okay, sure. It doesn't mean it's easy, but they pretty much get to work. You can practically see them clocking in and clocking out. The important thing is, not to treat them like it's something easy."

"You're lucky. You get to be around famous people all day."

He laughed. "They're not always famous. Sometimes I have to leave and go home before I remember how famous they are."

"How do you know that's the truth?"

"What?"

"When you have to go home to remember how famous they are."

"I don't know. That part's easy with kids. There's a lot that's hard about them, but that part's easy. They're always famous when I go home."

"I wish there were something that was always famous when I

got home."

He wanted to tell her that there was, but it was the kind of thing, if you were going to say it, you ought to say what it was. Still he went ahead.

"There is," he said.

"What is it?" she said.

"I don't know," he said.

It was his third time in Alice Peru's bed, and he had liked the other two times and he liked the thought of there being a fourth time and he liked very much to think of the kids and remember them afterwards while she took a shower. But he'd lied when he told her he didn't know. He'd lied because it was easier to embrace and to be in bed together again if they both didn't know what the famous thing was past childhood. But his conscience got the better of him as he was putting on his clothes a little later, because it looked like she knew that he knew what it was that kept people famous, and she knew it herself, and once it got to that point, things just felt bad if no one said it out loud, and he understood clearly that if he said it, it might mean there wouldn't be a fourth time in her bed, or, at the very least it opened up the real question of it, but it just felt too bad if it was there in the room but nobody said it. It felt the way it did when two kids who'd had some kind of fight both wanted there to be a sorry in the room but neither one of them wanted to say it, and he'd learned to be a genius of that moment, telling them that they might both feel better if they apologize, and there was no way to remember that now without telling her the truth.

"I lied. I *do* know what it is that can stay famous when you get home. It's love."

She looked at him and smiled. "Thanks for saying it."

"You're welcome," he said. And there was nothing to do then but to say goodbye to Alice Peru and go home.

THE DEAL

In all of America, there was finally one guy who understood that the point of living in a place was to write about it with a sense of its beauty, and even though it was Saturday night and in the place where he lived, a boy of seventeen was not supposed to spend that at home reading, Bahman Tabari lay in his bed with a book called *On the Road* by a man named Jack Kerouac. There was hope for Americans. They didn't make a specialty of disregarding the world around them. One of them at least, was paying close attention.

Let them go wherever they wanted to go on Saturday night, he thought. He was going to read and find a better America than the one available to him tonight. They *thought* they had something by going wherever they were going tonight, but he would take an America of forty years ago if it was actually being lived in right. Because the one of forty years ago made him dream of the one he wanted to live in, one where a man's capacity for a poetic reception of America was the primary thing about him.

An Iranian boy had to make use of whatever source he had. He wasn't going to learn from his mother and father. They filled the American absence of poetry with memories of home. He was going to have to accelerate his learning, which meant some Saturday nights at home. The good thing about that was that his learning was all his own. The first Tabari in history to dream of driving through the Rocky Mountains. The first one to dream of the diner he would stop in along the way.

Let me have a chance at *that* America, he thought. Not the one here at home, with its endless predictability. Even the wildness of the kids was predictable, because they weren't reaching for anything beautiful in their wildness, just for wildness itself.

The phone rang and he heard his mother answer it.

"Bahman," she called. "It's Johnny."

"Tell him I'm not home."

He heard his mother say that he would call him in a few minutes and then she came into his room.

"Why don't you talk to him?"

"I know what he's going to say. He's going to say that everybody is going to go see the new movie. I'm reading."

"Bahman," she said.

It hurt her to think of a boy alone in America and alone on Saturday night. He couldn't stand it.

"Why don't you want to see it?"

"It's the same as everything, Maman," he said. "It's in a big theater. It's got explosions. It's America. Who cares?"

She looked like she was going to cry.

"Why do you say these things? This is what the boys do. You are a boy."

"I'm not like them. You want to know what's going to happen? The good guys are going to win. You want to know how? Just barely. Who would have ever thought it?"

"Bahman," she said.

Jesus, he thought. She knows I'm right. That was the worst part of it, she knew he was right, but the boys had called him up to see a movie and it was Saturday night and they were in America and this was what you did. But he couldn't say to his mother—I'm working on it. I'm working on *my* America. Not this one where everyone does the predictable thing and goes to a predictable movie. He couldn't explain to her about Jack Kerouac and the diner along the way. He couldn't tell her he *knew* that diner, he knew the poetic element it was constituted of. It happened that he didn't know he knew until he'd started the book, but now he knew it for sure. But he would just look more lonely to her. Lonely and ridiculous. There's no loneliness when you're finding the angle with which you want to see America, he wanted to tell her. But she couldn't see how far-thinking his approach was.

"You can read tomorrow," she said.

"I am reading tonight."

"What if they don't call you next time?"

"Then they don't call me. Then I don't find out if the superhero wins or not."

His mother stood in his room, wishing he would go with the other boys.

"You are going to need more than books."

He smiled.

"You think so?"

"Yes," she said. "You laugh about it now."

He really laughed, then.

"Of course I laugh, Maman," he said. "You know the movie is terrible. You know what it's like there—everybody thinking that this is what a Saturday night is all about. You don't like that stuff any more than I do."

"It is different," she said. "You are a boy here. You know the other boys. You can talk with them and laugh with them. We had our time. We had our time in Iran when we were young. But you are just a boy."

"Maman," he said, nice and easy. "I'm learning." He held up the book to her. "These American writers show me more than those kids do."

He thought she would see they were on the same page—she wanted him to build a life in America, and he wanted to do that with a spirit that looked at America sadly and beautifully. A writer named Jack Kerouac knew it and the kids at school didn't. Bahman knew it didn't look like he was building something, but he was. Those kids going to the movie weren't *planning* their America. They were taking the one that was given. But they were going to look up one day and wonder what this place was, too. All he was doing was preparing for that moment. And he wasn't preparing with an answer; he was preparing with an approach, a feeling, a way of moving through. Something got lost there in a movie theater, something that didn't have room to breathe as everyone reverted to some kind of view that the new movie was the place to be. His mother must understand that, he thought. She knew what it was to feel lost here. Just because Johnny or any of the other boys called his house didn't mean he wasn't desperate for some kind of sign that America was more than its predictabilities. If there was a writer who was able to provide it, that was nothing to take lightly.

He showed her the book again. "This helps me more than all those kids," he said.

His mother looked down. "I feel very bad when you say that. I feel like you hate this country."

Good Lord, he thought. Here he was dreaming of the Rocky Mountains, and his mother was telling him he hated the country.

He couldn't stand it.

"When I was your age in Iran, I would give anything to go to the movies with my friends."

Something about that did it, and he thought—Sure. Of course, you did. But I'm here. Do you know how much you have to squeeze to find somebody who cares about *how* they are looking at the world here? You have to look all through your school and then you have to come up empty and you have to go to the public library and overhear a man say to the librarian that they only have one book by Jack Kerouac in the whole library, and you have to hear a kind of heartbreak in his voice, and then you have to go and find out what that one book is, if he's going to say it like that.

There had been a lot of America in that moment.

But his mother was like everybody else—they measured a guy's participation in America the wrong way. They measured it by what they could see. The movies on Saturday night were easy to see. They were *too* easy, Bahman thought. What he liked was the idea that it took some *work* to be a part of America, some solitary work, or inward, at least. They wanted everything to be easy. But what if you felt most American in your loneliness, at least if American meant looking at Americans sympathetically? It was just like this fellow Kerouac was saying—they were all trying. He wondered if Johnny and those other boys were trying, and he knew they were, but it was the way they tried: loud, desperate, looking for any chance of mockery they could get.

"Okay, Maman, I'll go," he said. "I'll call him back and I'll go."

"That's good," his mother said. "You are a boy like them."

"But we have to make some kind of deal," he said.

"What is it?" she said.

"You have to promise I'm never going to look lonely to you if I'm reading," he said.

"It is Saturday night," his mother said.

"Doesn't matter. This is more important than Saturday night. You have to promise you won't think I must be lonely if I'm reading. And that I must not be building for the future if I'm doing that. I'm going to need this book more than I'm going to need those guys. I know it is sad to hear that, but it is true. I know it might look to you like Americans have America as easy as one-two-three, and that all I have to do is go to the movies with them and I'll have it, too. But that's not how it works, Maman. I don't know how it works, but it's not like that. You have to promise, when you see me reading, you'll know I'm trying to figure it out."

"Okay," she said. "I promise."

His mother looked as sad as when she thought he wouldn't go.

"Look," he said. "I'm going. I'm going and I don't even know if the good guys are going to win. Could be anybody. Who knows?"

His mother smiled a little, and he saw she was smiling tearfully.

"Look," he said. "You're right. I can read tomorrow. It's Saturday night and there's a movie. I'll tell you about it tomorrow. Maybe the bad guys will win."

"I don't want you to go if you think it is stupid."

He laughed. "Don't worry about that. It's too funny to be stupid." It *was* too funny, but the humor of it was all his own. It was American and Iranian, and it gave him a glimpse of how to take in both. He couldn't run from the things that made his mother cry, and he couldn't run from the things that made her not cry, either. It was funny alright.

Along the way, they could make a deal. It seemed like a fair one. And he felt ready to hold up his end of it. He looked forward to holding it up tomorrow when he returned to the book, and he went to call Johnny on the phone.

THE NEW MAN

The New Man sat over the proceedings like a kind and friendly ghost, like somebody who was not only new but also old, because of how the people were like children before him. And maybe he *was* old, because the thing they were there to talk about fighting, the thing that the man whose face was on the tee-shirts had fought, the face that was staring at all of beauty and tragedy at once, which everybody in the room was staring at, too, even if they didn't do it all the time like he did—that thing they were all against could seem like *it* was what was new, sometimes. It had been growing over their lives, for one thing, or trying to at least. And it knew how to present itself with a shine and sparkle of the kind that wasn't there in the room, with its plain walls and plain chairs and plain food and plain clothes on the people, though there was a different kind of shine and sparkle in there, one that came out slowly and broadly and deeply.

The New Man sat and listened along with everyone else as the speaker spoke of the man whose face was on the tee-shirts, how he had not wanted his struggle to be a struggle of death, he had wanted it to be a struggle of life. He had wanted it to be so much a struggle of life that one small country had not been enough for him, one large continent had not been enough for him, it had taken the thought of a whole new man to be enough for him, one who stared at all of beauty and tragedy at once, and who said that whatever was to come was in his hands. The New Man sat and nodded, and the people felt him nodding.

A young woman who had just graduated from college made

a space available inside herself for the New Man, but she did it begrudgingly, because of how it was the man again, same as always, and she was beginning to feel more and more that it was a New Woman who was going to have to come along for the world to be what it could be. She didn't even *know* what it could be, but she still knew that. And she didn't intend for the New Woman to be walking alongside the New Man. She would be leading sometimes, and he would be leading sometimes, and sometimes both of them would be and sometimes neither. What she felt begrudging about was the way the story was already about him before anything had even happened yet. And even a great man like him hadn't looked around and said, What can I already learn from women and what they have already been doing, before I go off making declarations about the New Man. As far as she knew, at least. As far as the story was told. And she could hear the voices of men saying, This isn't a matter of what can I learn from, this is a matter of guns and bullets. And she said to them, Who made it a matter of guns and bullets? I am just as unafraid of guns and bullets as you, but I know how to be unafraid without letting my own language be the language of guns and bullets. Be glad that I am making a space inside myself for the New Man. Be glad, and make a space inside yourself for the knowledge that I knew the New Man before he knew himself.

A middle-aged man who had come to the place by himself and would be going home by himself, bowed his head as he listened and thought of how much he had lost on account of the New Man. He had lost a family and friends. He had lost a country and a sense of home. And still, he felt a great gratitude towards the New Man, as he thought of how much worse it would have been if he had never known him, if he had never known the *need* for him, if he had never known he had a right to believe in the need for him. He could have been like all those men he had worked side-by-side with who had found a new man in a bottle each night for years. He didn't know if it was pride or sorrow that kept them away from rooms like this, but he wished they could see how it was, how it didn't matter if the room was full or if there were just a couple of people. Either way, there was a newness that was something lasting, not something to wake up with a headache with the next day. And he couldn't shake the feeling that all those he had lost, people and countries, were going to be among the last to know. They were going to be the last to know about the New Man, and in a way, he was one of them and in a way, he was not. But he knew that when he listened to talk of him, he felt like he was on a bridge to somewhere. He couldn't tell where the bridge was going, but he knew he had left the place where he was and he had an honest view of the world a man could have from up there.

An elderly woman sitting in the back smiled and felt very happy during the whole of the speech. She felt a great affection for the New Man, without a concern for the specifics of his presence or lack thereof. He had come and he hadn't come at all. The whole thing was poetry to her, either way. It was beautiful to have lived as long as she had and walk into a place where poetry was at hand like that. It was beautiful to see all the different people there and to think of them engaged in the same efforts she had been engaged in. She felt good about what she had achieved in her own life, and she felt glad to still have some people to remember those days with, not for the remembering itself, but for the being who she was. It had gotten easier as she had gotten older to be who she was, and she knew that was not necessarily how it always was. It could have gotten harder, and if she had not been thinking of the New Man, it would have been. If she had turned away from the world and tried to see only what she had to see, she would never have even *known* who she was, and she could listen to the speaker now and silently thank the New Man and not miss a word.

The young man listening and thinking of his father was a writer, and being a writer, he thought of a book. It was a book written by the man whose face was on the tee-shirts, and it was a book of poetry and a book about guns and bullets. His father had found it and secretly brought it into their country at a time when the book was against the law to have. I would like to write something like that, he thought, something a man would be willing to risk his liberty to have. And if I wrote it, it would have the same elements that book had. I would have to go to the same places as a writer that a revolutionary went to when he went to guerrilla warfare. Which was why it was beautiful to sit there and listen to talk of the New Man and think of his father, but it was a beauty he would have to keep going on his own somehow when the talk ended and everyone went back out to the street.

The talk ended and everyone went back out to the street, where it was the same Old Man, the same Old Man on a Saturday night, which meant heights and depths, and, same as always, he looked new among the heights and old among the depths, but the people coming out of the room were carrying something that could see past that, as well. They were carrying the New Man as well, and whether he was actually New or Old, they were carrying him like a friend. The young woman and the middle-aged man and the elderly woman felt the night become a little more their own, and the young man who was a writer felt it become a little more *his* own, though he felt it become a little less his own, too, as he looked around and thought of everyone he would never know, everyone who was trying just as hard as he was, whether they were writers or not, whether they were revolutionaries or not, and he only knew he needed them, he needed every single one of them, seen or unseen, known or unknown, because he could not be himself without them. He could not be who *he* was without them, and he still had great respect and admiration for the New Man, but he was also trying to have great respect and admiration for himself.

Ernesto "Che" Guevara, he said, I love you, and I love my father, and I love the New Man, but I have to love the old one in front of me. I have to love him even if it means walking down the street by myself again in order to do it. It may mean I won't be making any new systems of government or economics or even society, but I will still be telling man something new about himself, and in that, I am with you, I am with your being willing to die for the New Man, and I am with my father and *his* being willing to die for him, too, and anybody can look at me and say—what are you talking about, being willing to die when all you are doing is walking down the street and going home and writing stories about it?—and all I can tell you is that I love him, too. I love whoever is saying that, too, because of the way that he fits into the world in front of me, which is the only one I have, and I can't live believing there are those whose lives should be ending in that world I should be seeking, in order to make a better one. Ernesto "Che" Guevara, I believe in the truth of your fight and I love you, but I see the New Man everywhere I look, I see him everywhere in the old one, otherwise I wouldn't be a writer, I wouldn't be trying to tell him each day that I see him, that he is the hardest-working and longest-suffering man I have ever seen, and if he is willing to listen, I think some good will come of that.

Upstairs, the New Man stayed until everyone had left, and he was about to leave himself, when the woman who swept up came to work. He sat down and watched her, and when he saw the necklace she wore around her neck, he knew that if there were any presence that was there in the room with her, it wasn't him. It wasn't him, but that was alright. He didn't feel the slightest bit insulted, and he felt only a great respect and admiration for how she worked. He watched as she picked up a flyer with a picture of the face on it. He watched her stare at the picture, thinking of the man who was from the same part of the world as she was, and feeling very proud of him, and he watched her be unable to throw it away, putting it in her pocket instead, to do something big with it later.

BEE ON A STRING

What we would do was, we would catch the bees while they were inside a flower, using a plastic bag, and we would take them and put them in the freezer at Marcus's house, and Marcus's mother didn't like it but she didn't stop us—she seemed to think there were worse things twelve- and thirteen-year-old boys could be doing, which was true, though probably not from the bees' perspective. Ten minutes in the freezer was about the right length of time, and we would take them out, and while they were alive but still, we would tie one end of a piece of string around their bodies. Something wonderful would happen—the bee would move a leg, and then an antenna and then its whole body would start to beat again, and it would get its wings back, and then we could honestly say we had done something with a warm day in late spring, which was, we had gotten ourselves a bee on a string.

If we had been poets instead of twelve- and thirteen-year-old boys, we might've tried to write something about how nice it was there in Marcus's garden with the bees buzzing among his mother's flowers and no expectations of us anywhere in the world on a Saturday near the end of the school year, except our own expectation to make the day last as long as it could. We recognized the way the bees and their activity contributed to that feeling, and we wanted to do something about that. A poet can do that with a poem, but a boy is in need of more direct action. They were the ones who really understood nature, the bees were, because they could combine the beauty of the day with work, and we wanted to get some kind of access to that realm, and even though we would have admitted that what we were producing wasn't as good as honey, we still thought it was pretty good.

A bee on a string. It looked to us as much like the start of summer as anything else could.

It must've looked like something to John Vasilias, who came to take Marcus's sister, Sarah, down to the lake. The three of us: me, Marcus, and Arijit, each holding one end of a string and trying to avoid the other. It took your full concentration. You didn't want to let go, but the bees would catch on that the thing at the other end of the string was something they could sting. It was because we were focusing so hard that we felt like we could get a little smart-alecky with John Vasilias. He was the guy who, whenever I was playing basketball in my backyard and I heard a car going fast down Hedgebrook with loud music playing, I assumed was him. He scared us all a little.

"How did you do that?" he said to us.

"We caught 'em," Marcus said.

"We lassoed 'em," Arijit said.

"We're bee wranglers."

"Yee-haw!"

We didn't look directly at him the whole time. We couldn't really afford to. It took a special kind of dance to hold the string and avoid the bee. John Vasilias could see that himself. I couldn't think of any other circumstance under which we could have been smart-alecky with him. Anywhere else, it would have been our demise. But we had the bees on our side. And by extension, everything else about the warm day that went with them.

John Vasilias was thrown, but he got his bearings back when

Sarah came outside. I had to admit that going down to the lake with her looked like a pretty nice thing to do with a warm day, too.

She shook her head and smiled when she saw us. "Don't get stung," she said.

Arijit and I both turned to her to smile back, but we had gotten too close to each other and, in that momentary lapse in our concentration, our bees flew toward each other and tangled their strings. We both tried to untangle at the same time, but as we got closer to each other it got worse, and meanwhile the bees were still coming in our direction, until there was nothing to do but let go and watch them fly off together in the sky, where they still had their strings tangled but at least they had each other.

"I guess you'll have to lasso some new ones," said John Vasilias.

"I guess so," Arijit said. He and I looked at each other. Marcus was still wrangling his bee, but he paused to look in our direction.

"I'm starting to feel bad about it," Arijit said. He and I looked at Marcus. If we were going to be suddenly struck with sympathy for the bees, we had to give it some direction.

"But you guys are bee wranglers," John Vasilias said.

"Yes, but what did those bees ever do to us?"

"Come on, John," said Sarah. "Let's go."

"I just want to see them lasso one bee."

The one time in our lives when we could treat John Vasilias as an equal, that we could mess with him a little bit, as if we were all of an equal standing, and here it was slipping away from us. A guy like that was very aware of his standing, too. I thought of the two bees who had flown away with their strings tangled. I wished I was one of them.

Arijit took a new piece of string and tied a little loop in it. John Vasilias watched closely. I thought what a crazy thing a guy's standing was. Here he could go down to the lake with Marcus's sister on a nice day, but instead he was watching us kids messing around with bees in the garden. Then again, if he had just left, we would've told everyone about how we'd fooled him. That was pretty much certain.

"Sometimes it works and sometimes it doesn't," Arijit said.

He lowered the string into a flower where a bee was.

"Come on, John," said Sarah. "I've seen them do it."

"You have?" John Vasilias said.

"Yes. He's right. Sometimes it works and sometimes it doesn't. But I want to go to the lake."

There was a look in her eyes just after she said it. She glanced at us, and it was very quick, but I was sure I saw it. It was a look that said, I'm not *always* going to like guys like John Vasilias. It was as though she wanted us to know. And I felt sorry for him just then. He wasn't a bad guy. He just relied too much on standing. If he hadn't been like that, we might not have tried to fool him in the first place.

"You've seen them do it?" he said.

"Yes. Let's go. Everybody's already down there."

You could tell he didn't want to go yet, that he wasn't sure how the whole thing was going to affect his standing.

I tried to look quiet, like I wasn't planning on telling anybody, which really I wasn't. It had been enough to see Marcus's sister give us a look like that.

"I think it's pretty stupid," John Vasilias said.

None of us said anything. It certainly didn't feel like anything worth arguing about. John Vasilias and Sarah got in the car. He turned the music on loud and they drove off so fast the tires screeched.

We didn't catch any more bees after that. Marcus cut the string from his and it flew off into the sky. We sat on the grass and watched the bees among the flowers. Maybe there would be a time when we would find something else to do about how nice they looked, but we didn't know what it was yet.

We tried playing basketball, but it was too hot, and as soon as one guy made a lazy move, the others would feel lazier too, so Arijit and I decided to walk home.

That was what I was really looking forward to, because I wanted to ask Arijit if he'd seen the look on Marcus's sister's face. I couldn't believe she even cared what we thought, but it had seemed in that moment, she did. I guessed there must have been *something* about John Vasilias she liked. But a guy ought to be able to let some kids call themselves bee wranglers for a minute, even if it wasn't right to stick those bees in the freezer to do it. We would've told him the truth if he would have let us have the joke.

It wasn't until we started walking that I realized that at the heart of it was girls and the mystery of why they liked who they liked. We couldn't open that up between us because it would be like floating off into some vast and endless sky. So, we turned to something more certain and we talked about where those two bees on strings were by now.

ARGENTINA VERSUS FRANCE

"Argentina is going to play France," the mother said.

The father did not look up.

"Will you call him?"

"He does not want to talk to us," the father said.

Argentina was going to play France, and the people of Argentina were going to pour their hearts out for Argentina, and the people of France were going to pour their hearts out for France, and somehow their boy was going to say that *his* heart was something that could only pour out to himself, just as he had when he'd left their town, saying that all he saw around him was death. They wanted to call him up and say, Can you imagine the people of Argentina today, can you imagine the people of France, just as they did at every World Cup, dreaming of the places and the people. They were not American, so they did not see those places as *foreign* the way Americans did. They saw them as places and people they could've been, at least the poor countries, and they all wanted the poor countries to win when they faced a rich country, but even so, they respected the hearts of the people in the rich countries, since there was space for them to come out, too.

They would not say they did not care that Argentina was going to play France. They would still watch the game on their television. But they would not feel the way they wanted to feel.

The way they wanted to feel was that they knew the world. They knew Argentina and they knew France. That was what the game did for them. They both tried to live in a way that knew those places the rest of the time too, but the game made it easy. It made it effortless. But how could you know the world when you did not know your own son? They did not see the death he saw all around him in their town. If there was a time when they could've seen it, they did not remember. Was it an American death? Their boy had grown up here. Maybe that was what was needed to see it.

"Do you think he will watch the game?" the mother said. She already knew he would not. He hadn't been able to watch the crowds when he had been home, even on television. He said that he couldn't stop thinking about all of them.

They are just people, the mother and father had said. They are going to watch the game and then they are going to go home.

They could not get at what made the boy dissatisfied about that.

Who did he want to be? they thought. Did he want to have a world that was bigger than that of the World Cup? How did you do that? Where could you go?

He had told them he had to go back to his little room in the city. Where he did not have a television. He had not said to them that he felt their lives were small, but they wanted to say to him, It is the World Cup, a time when we feel big, a time when we can all feel big.

"Maybe he will watch it," the mother said. "Maybe he will go to someone's house and watch it. Or one of the places where they are showing the game."

It was nice to think they could call him up afterwards and say: The game! Imagine the hearts today of the people of Argentina! Imagine the hearts of the people of France! They were places the mother and father could not imagine anymore that they would ever go, but they could go there when the boy's heart went with them. They were not far from the people of Argentina and France then.

And the boy had been a great one to go to those places with, before he had started to feel this way. He would go quietly, but he would go. Suddenly in his quietude he would say something to make them realize he was thinking very hard about Argentina and France, as the homes of the people he shared the world with.

He had told them he couldn't share it like this anymore. But they didn't understand. What could he be sharing with anybody in his little room? What did he expect to find? The whole world was waking up to the thought of Argentina versus France. It would be one thing if he said the problem was America. They could understand that. They could talk about their own problems here. But the distance the boy felt from their town was the same distance he felt from them, and it was a lonely and heartbroken feeling to be thrown in with America like that. They were the three who had come here together, after all. Their girl had been born here. But they were the three who had started the adventure together.

"If I knew he would watch it, I would feel better," the mother said. "I would say, okay, he was unhappy here, but it is because our town is small and he is young and the city is big. But what is bigger than Argentina against France?"

"There is something," the father said.

The mother did not know if she wanted to hear what that thing was. She had not been expecting an answer.

"He wants to see if he can get there on his own."

"He has already been there now for a while."

"Not the city. I don't mean the city. He wants to see if he can go to the place of Argentina against France. To that thing we feel when we see Argentina versus France, when we see the people and we see that for everything else, they are still the people with whom we are alive. Do you know how it is when you are watching the game and you feel very close to the people of Argentina and to the people of France? He is trying to do that by himself, without the game."

The mother was scared to hear it. Why would he want to do that by himself when they had the game together? They were a family, and they were from one of the poor countries themselves, and if they did not have the World Cup, she did not know what they had. They were already lost in America. They were already on their own when it came to being a spirit on earth, to being more than their weekly earnings and paycheck. The mother secretly believed America would never be great at soccer because it did not believe in being great at anything it was not already great at from the start. The people were too sure in their belief that they were already at the top at birth. Still, they were here, and they had a life here. But if they could not be a family together during the World Cup, during the time when the world was in charge, not America, when the *language* of the story of the world did not have to be the language of America in order for the story to count, then she just did not know when they could feel like a family again.

A man wasn't *supposed* to do that by himself, she thought. It was too much for one person. At least if she knew he was watching the game today, then she would know he was still aiming for something familiar. She imagined him walking through the empty streets of the city while the whole world was inside with the game. The father understood, she thought, insofar as he thought it was just a stage.

But what if it was not a stage? You could not disconnect yourself in a country where there was so much disconnection. You had to soak up the moments of connection, like it was water in a desert. But here the boy was, saying he could not watch the game because all he could think about was everybody's lives, and when he got that way, all he could do was go outside and walk.

In her sorrow, she wondered what he expected to find out there. It was the same old America that had to be told about the beauty of the world.

"It is America," she said. "Back home, he would not go off to the city like this. He would be here to watch the game with us. He would understand about Argentina against France."

"I don't know," the father said. "I don't know if it is America. Maybe back home he would be here with us, but I don't know."

The mother knew she was grasping, but it felt good to blame the one country that she felt would never win the World Cup, that it felt good to watch go out each time because of the way it won at everything else.

"Anyway, it doesn't matter," the father said. "We are here. He grew up here. We have to remember he is not disregarding Argentina against France. I don't understand *how*, but he is looking for something that is in those countries too, when he goes out and walks through the city. It is there during the World Cup and it is there the rest of the time too. A young man has to look, I suppose. I am like you. I am scared of what he will find. I am scared because for me it is easy—turn on the game and watch the beauty of the players' motion. Watch the beauty of their hearts in action. I know there will be goals. Each of those goals will be *my* heart in action.

That is how I can go to Argentina and France. But he goes inside himself."

The mother felt that she was going to cry. "We had always gone together," she said. "He is going where he can only go by himself. We used to go together and we would find the whole world there. Even America. But I don't want to go without him. I don't want to go if it is without the boy."

"No," the father said. "It is not right. We have to watch the game. We have to believe he will come back to it. He will go all over the world in his mind, but he will come back to a thing like the way they are kicking the ball on the grass in Argentina and in France. And in our country. And in America, too. Somehow, we have to believe it. He will see that it is still these simple little things. Maybe it *is* America. Maybe it is America that makes him reach for something way up in the sky, away from us and away from everything. I don't know. But he will come back to it."

The mother still believed that none of this would have happened if they still lived in a country that loved soccer. That breathed soccer. Where the people knew where to look for beauty––amongst themselves, amongst each other, not somewhere far and above and out. Those were their people. If the boy had grown up among them, he would know that he did not have to carry the weight of what he was looking for by himself.

She thought she would cry at the sight of the teamwork of both countries. It made her think of the boy. He had never wanted anything for himself. He had never been occupied with the things boys were occupied with. But he had always cared about the game. He had always watched it in a way that took in the world.

"We have to watch it," the father said. "Because he will come back. Right now, soccer is not enough for him. He needs something more direct. He needs to see Argentina and France in the faces of the people. I don't mean the people from those places. I mean the thing in their faces that is in those places. That is how I understand it, at least. That is what I think he was trying to tell us. He did not hate the crowds at the game. But he needed to see them one by one. I don't know how long he will need to do that. But we have to believe he will come back to it. And we have to believe that when he does, he may say, what about Argentina versus France? What about that game? We have to be ready for it. We have to be ready to tell him all about it."

And, as she had known somewhere inside she would do all along, the mother turned on the game.

YOUNG AND OLD

"I've got my rules," Eddie was saying. "You can't work on a street like this without some rules. They're going to fight. If I came here thinking I was going to break up every fight, I wouldn't last long."

He was talking to the young man. The young man was on his way to declare his love for an older woman. She was twelve years older. He was going to tell her he didn't care about any of that. He liked listening to Eddie because it made him feel older.

"If it's in the bar, that's my job. If it's on the sidewalk in front of the bar, that's my job, too. If it's in front of one of these other places, and it looks like it's going to *stay* over there, I just let it go."

The young man felt good to hear that some of the fights Eddie had to just let go. He understood it. He felt sure the woman would see he was one of those young men who were older than their years.

"Now if it's across the *street*, then I've got a front row seat. I'm going to be on this stool right here. Because suppose I see something over there and walk across the street and then something starts up inside over here. Who's going to be out of a job? Me. This one time there was a fight across the street and a drunk woman comes running out of Max's to yell at me for not going over there to break it up. They think you're some superhero or something. There are no superheroes. People are going to fight. After a while, you start to see the look in their eyes as soon as they come into the bar."

The young man wanted to tell the woman about Eddie. Listen, he would say, I'm trying to do my best in a world with no superheroes.

"Some guys, you see them come in, and you think, damn, I

hope he finds some girl to talk to. And *then* you think, I hope the girl he talks to doesn't leave him to talk to somebody else. After a while, you start to see they're bringing the fight with them. They're bringing it from their own lives. A girl starts talking to somebody else. Okay. You can start talking to somebody else too, right? But they think they've found their fight. They think a fight is what they came out to look for. That's why it gets old after a while. It gets old to see a guy think he's tough after a couple of beers. It's new to *him*, but it's old to me."

The young man believed it was old to him, too.

"So now the thing I've figured out is to be proactive about it. You know what that means? You'll never guess. Friendliness. I never would've guessed it either. Friendliness is the most intimidating force in the world, because they don't want to see what it looks like when you stop being their friend. They need to know you are choosing to be their friend, so if the need arises for you to be something other than that, you are prepared. Anyway, it's better for me too. It keeps me from feeling old and weary about how they're always going to fight. Even though they're always going to fight. Friendliness is what keeps you young. You just got to be ready for the other thing."

The young man thought it wasn't very old of him to want to prove he wasn't young. He ought to go to see the woman as though he hadn't given a second thought to being twelve years younger, as though he had barely noticed it. But there were a million things he liked about her being older. He was going to have to tell her he liked those things while also showing that he barely noticed it.

He said goodbye to Eddie and left.

When he walked back three hours later, he actually did feel old, because now he had a broken heart. She had told him that maybe if he were four or five years older and she were four or five years younger, that would be one thing, but that at twenty-six and thirty-eight, they were in two different worlds. He had said maybe that was true for some twenty-six and thirty-eight-year-olds, but it wasn't true of them, and she had softened, but she hadn't softened enough. She had only softened enough to make his walk back something soft and quiet, and not angry, though he still felt a great resentment toward time for not working with him on this one.

He was lost in a soft and quiet resentment as he walked back, and then he saw a commotion across the street from Eddie's bar and then he looked over at Eddie's stool and he did not see Eddie.

He was in the middle of it, across the street.

When he saw the young man, Eddie pulled himself out of the fray, seeming to remember his job, and he explained it as they walked back across the street together.

"It was a couple of guys coming out of Delaney's. Same as always. Like I've seen a hundred times. But then do you know what somebody did?" Eddie said. He was furious in a way that looked young, and the young man thought it was beautiful. "Somebody on the corner there, they took out their phone and started *filming* it. They were just walking by, they weren't even in the place with them. They started filming somebody else's fight, so they could take it home with them. I wanted to take their phone and smash it."

"I've seen how people do that," the young man said.

"A fight," Eddie said. "Sure, it's stupid. Sure, it's probably over some dumb thing. But you've got to have some respect for it, still.

They're still trying. It's a stupid kind of trying but it's still trying. I wanted to smash the guy's phone so he would never try that again. Jesus. What do they think this street is? What do they think anything is?"

Eddie had told him once that he was fifty-four years old, but the young man thought that he had never seen him look so young as when he felt like the world had become a place where a guy would pull out a phone and film a fight on the corner. It was a way he hoped he would be furious about some things when he was older. And he gave up on thinking about being young and being old for the night and he tried to remember the woman's face when she softened, and Eddie's expression when he was furious, and it was tiring enough being twenty-six, just like it probably was being any age.

JOE WEST'S BROTHER

"The beautiful thing about fighting fascism," eighty-nine-year-old Joe West was saying, "is that if you die, you die on the side of every work of art ever created, even the bad ones. You die on the side of every book and every song and every painting, and every one of them belongs to you now as a memorial and a remembrance."

We thought he was just being poetic.

"Listen," he said, "I'm not just trying to sound poetic. What does every book and every song and every painting say? It says I don't know, but here's something. What does fascism say? It doesn't even get to that. It says, I know."

Eighty-nine-year-old Joe West had a twinkle in his eye toward the rise of fascism in America. He looked like a little kid when he talked about it. I had to admit I'd asked Celine to the old black-and-white movie playing at the public library partly because I thought we could use a reminder.

"How'd you know?" Celine said to me.

"How'd I know what?"

"That this would be the best place to come."

"That's an easy one," I said. "Just go wherever they're giving something away for free."

"I don't know about countries," Joe West said. "Remember that America took its time to say anything about Hitler and Mussolini and those guys. The most reliable enemy fascism has ever had has been art."

"He's a writer," Celine said, nudging me.

"Then you're a soldier," Joe West said.

"I don't know about that."

"Yes, you do. It's alright. Modest soldiers are the best kind. We're going to need you, you know."

I had to admit it was nice to be needed. I hadn't heard that a lot. But I didn't want to write like I thought I was needed. I wanted to keep writing like the world was acting like it didn't need writers but secretly it did.

I didn't want to write like fascism was a target exactly, either. I just wanted to aim for people, and figured if I did that, fascism would look very small along the way.

I wanted to write like one man, perhaps even Joe West himself, was bigger than all of fascism.

We settled in for a black-and-white movie from a time when people were thinking of fascism a great deal. I thought of all those people who'd watched it back then and I got more wrapped up in them than in the movie, which seemed like a pretty anti-fascist way to watch it, to tell the truth.

"What if fascism is just an angry way to be sad?" I said.

"Shhh," Celine said.

I thought about how important it was to have a sad way to be sad, though I didn't want to discount the importance of having an angry way to be angry. The characters in the movie seemed to agree.

I don't think we're going to out-anger the fascists, I thought We may out-sad them, but I don't know if that wins you anything.

I believed Joe West when he said fighting fascism was on the side of every work of art ever created, but weren't people just going to get tired of art again and want something clean and simple and straight, even if it was a lie? Even if it was a very big lie, because the truth was so sprawling and unkempt? You could walk past the library and see all the life in the books, or you could walk past it and see a building, but one of those wore you out more than the other.

Before we left, I asked Joe West how he knew all that. He was staying behind to put the chairs away.

"My brother," he said. "He died in the Spanish Civil War. 1937. When I read a good book, I see him. When I hear a good song, I see him."

"I wonder if he saw him during the movie," Celine said, after we left.

"Hell," I said—which was not directed at her but at the world, which she knew, which was another thing I liked about her—"He must have seen him. *I* saw him, and I didn't even know the guy."

A GOOD NEIGHBORHOOD

Some of the people at William T. Ford Real Estate looked happy to have a black man join the company, and Peter Willis recognized their happiness for what it was: They were happy about themselves. Look at us, they thought. Have you ever seen such a magnanimous collection of people? But he thought it was a harmless look, and he had wanted a job where he could be in motion after six years at a department store, and so he smiled back at them.

He liked the independence of the job. They had an office meeting on Monday mornings, but after that he was on his own.

It was hard to get business at first, but he believed that if they gave him a chance, a house was a thing he could sell. He could think about family, about his own family, and he could put that into his salesmanship. He knew what a family could do with a house. He knew from thinking of his own mother and father how much of a shelter they could make. And that got into the house itself. It got into the building, into the rooms and walls. He could walk into an empty house and see the possibility, and it was something much more than selling ties and shirts and suits.

Once a week for several hours, each agent was in charge of answering the calls that came in. When Peter heard the other agents on the phone, he would often hear them tell somebody that a particular house was in a good neighborhood. They only mentioned the neighborhood if it was a good neighborhood. He noticed that an agent who had been telling a prospective client about a good neighborhood usually was not quick to smile at him or say hello the rest of the day.

The men and women at William T. Ford Real Estate had been talking about houses being in good neighborhoods for so long, they had almost forgotten what it meant. They felt their magnanimity beginning to fade because having a black man at the office reminded them what it meant, and they did not like that. Instead of recognizing they did not like that, they began to feel they did not like Peter Willis.

It was not racist, they felt. It was the way he moved through the office, or his voice or his general manner. Anyway, it was not their fault that prospective clients who called were interested in good neighborhoods.

The men and women who worked at William T. Ford Real Estate had every opportunity to go home and say to their wives and husbands, Something is wrong. Something is very wrong. There is not a single thing Peter Willis has done except to join our company, but in doing so, he's shown us something that was always there, and I hate that thing. I don't know what to do about that hate because if I open it up, I am going to find a lot more there than I knew. More than just my job and good neighborhoods, I am going to find more truths than I can bear, and I am afraid the thing I hate is so deep inside myself that it might as well *be* myself. If they had said it, their husbands and wives could have said, Yes. I know what you mean. I am afraid that I have that thing inside myself, too. I don't know what to do about it either. And they could have cried together, and they could have discovered that crying together is a good thing to do, at least at first. But none of that happened, and it didn't happen because the reality of what defined a good neighborhood was bigger in the lives of the William T. Ford agents than their imaginations. It was not that their imaginations were small. It was that they had grown used to using them to disappear. Not to appear more fully than they did before, even if that meant crying. A good neighborhood didn't *have* to be bigger than their imaginations, but it would mean going to some lost and unknown part of America to have it otherwise. It would mean going somewhere where they would have to use their imaginations to appear more than to disappear every day. If they were to face the way they had to look at themselves because of Peter Willis, it would not end with Peter Willis. Where would it end? They didn't know, and they could not embark upon something with no end, because they couldn't see how that could be good for anybody.

So instead, they saw Peter Willis as the cause of a problem, and that made sense to them because they had not thought about it before he had joined the company, and because that made the matter finite. They did not *feel* like they were repeating something very old in America. There was enough in their lives that was new, that felt new when they woke up each morning, that they thought their feelings about Peter Willis must be new, too. And if they were new, they were clean. It was a brand-new moment in the life of the world, and it didn't have to do with anything old. There were new houses being built and new houses being sold and new people looking to buy them, and they believed the things inside them to be just as new as those. Some of the William T. Ford agents were young and some of them were old and the young ones and the old ones held on to the newness of their feelings differently, with different levels of desperation, but they all believed them to be new.

The ones who had been happy to have a black man join

the company would go out in cars to meet prospective clients at houses for sale and they would tell them the house was in a good neighborhood, and they would come back to the office and see Peter Willis at his desk, and they would not be sure about the meaning of what they had just said, and they would not be sure about themselves. They had felt sure, driving back to the office. And they would have to work to remind themselves when they saw him that their feelings were new, and they did not like that. It was still better than calling their feelings old, but they did not like being caught between those two. They were the ones who had been working at William T. Ford for years and years. If anybody should feel caught between two bad options, they thought it should be Peter Willis. It wasn't the people who had put in the time and energy to make William T. Ford what it was. As their thoughts went back over the years, it did not occur to them that whoever had been the first black man or woman to work at William T. Ford Real Estate would have done something to the ease of talking about good neighborhoods. It did not occur to them that Peter Willis had come in and sat at his desk and started his job. They lost the ability to see it. And they lost the ability to see him. Men and women would look the other way when they passed by him. They would not talk with him. It did not feel to them like something old. The day was new, their listings were new, and their feelings about Peter Willis were new. If they were new, they were clean. They were not their parents, after all. They were born to go past their parents in the same way that white Americans were meant to go beyond their pasts. When they looked around, they felt like they had done it, and so there certainly couldn't be anything old in the way they looked at Peter Willis.

A GOOD NEIGHBORHOOD

For three weeks in a row, he was given the early-morning phone shift, the time when hardly anybody called. He knew what it was. And the people in the office knew he knew what it was, and yet it still felt new to them. It did not feel connected to anything anybody had ever done to anyone in the past. It was a wholly new day, and nobody had ever seen this moment of the world before.

It did not feel like something old to them when he began to lose his own smile at work, or when he began to walk through the hallway without saying hello to anyone. It was a new day, and if he couldn't see that, they didn't know what they could do about it. They knew it certainly could not be good for his salesmanship though, to be far away from his own smile like that.

Peter Willis lost the feeling he'd had around a house and what it could do. It was a building, with rooms and walls. He could not tell anybody a house was in a good neighborhood. He did not know what it meant.

He remembered the home his mother and father had made, in a neighborhood the people at William T. Ford would not have called a good neighborhood. His mother and father had made what happened *inside* the house their concern. A good neighborhood only went so far. You couldn't make a good city, a good country, or a good world. What could you make good? Where did you have a place with the *power* to make it good? You had yourself, they had told him.

What did they think, he thought, that a good neighborhood got you anyway, even if that was what it was? Did they think your work was done? Did they think inside of a house like that, you didn't have to still try? That you could just rest in the comfort of where you were, and you wouldn't feel like the questions life gave you required your best response? What kind of neighborhood was that? It was imaginary, is what it was. And you couldn't sell imaginary if you didn't believe in imaginary. It was sad to realize, because he believed he could sell a house. He believed he could do it his way.

Peter Willis stayed for four months at William T. Ford Real Estate. He got tired of the early-morning phone shift. He got tired of the way he was seen there and he got tired of hearing about good neighborhoods. The men and women at William T. Ford silently reverted to innocence. When he left, none of them went home and said, There is something in me I hate and this thing is very old. It is as old as America. I do not know how to be American without it. So, I do not know how to be alive without it. But it is not living. It is not living because when I put a wall between myself and another person, I put a wall between my heart and me. And I have gone a long time saying these walls are just walls, they are necessary to hold things up. But I do not know what it is I am holding up. Nobody asked me. They told me to live in fear of its collapse. They told me I was a good person for holding it up. But if we were good, we would look at each other as we did it. We would face each other and smile and laugh. I remember enough to know what it would feel like to be good. It would not feel like we each had to be behind our own walls to do it. There is still some way to be good without being afraid in America and I want to learn it.

THE OUTDOOR MOVIE

Armon Eskanderian didn't think there was anything strange about it at first when he asked Elyssa Green if she would like to see the outdoor movie with him at Rossi Park on Saturday night. He was glad she said yes. He got his hair cut on Wednesday, so it would have a few days to fit his head. It wasn't till Saturday afternoon that he remembered he hadn't gone to the outdoor movies to watch the movies that summer. He had gone to sit next to the big white wall of the County Fair Building on which the movies were projected and watch the faces of the people. He hoped she would like it as much as he did.

When they got there, he laid a blanket beside the wall of the County Fair Building.

"I forgot to mention," he said. "I don't come to watch the movies."

"What do you come for?" she said.

"To watch the people watching."

She fell in love with him. She sat down and tried to not show it on her face that she had fallen in love with him.

"What do you like about watching them?"

"They're honest," he said.

"What about the rest of the time?"

"The rest of the time? That's very far away, isn't it?"

She did not exactly fall out of love with him when he said that, but she saw she would not be able to be free with it.

It was nice that the moment before him was everything, but not so nice as to make everything else a secret.

At least he was honest from the start. She laughed and thought of how it seemed like it was always like this—the young men who dreamed couldn't let anyone in on their dreams, and the ones who didn't, could. The last boy she had known who had been able to tell her everything had been when she was fifteen. What happened to them in those next ten years to send the ones with dreams so far off the map? So far off to the side, they couldn't talk and love their way back? How was it she could see the beauty of watching the people watching but still be perfectly happy to sit among them and watch the movie, both?

"Have you been doing this all summer?" Elyssa said.

"Yes," Armon said.

"Don't the people mind?"

"Not anymore. They might have at first, but now they know I'm not going to do anything bad with it."

"With what?"

"With their expressions as they're watching."

Elyssa looked out at the crowd. He was right. Nobody seemed particularly bothered.

"What *are* you going to do with them?" she said.

"I don't know," he said. "Just hold them, I guess."

Some of them, she figured, were working so hard to know their own dreams they couldn't afford to stop and explain them. That was the generous way to look at it, but she felt like being generous just then.

The movie started, and they watched the faces. It was a romantic movie. There was joy and wonder and concern and worry and relief.

At one point, Elyssa looked over at Armon watching the people watch the movie.

"You like it over here, don't you?"

"Yes," he said. "Very much."

She smiled. "I'm going to go and sit with the people for a little bit," she said. "Just for a few minutes."

"Okay," he said.

Elyssa sat in the middle of the crowd and watched the movie. She liked the thought of Armon watching her, even if he was watching everybody. She liked being with them in his view. She liked who they became when he was watching them.

She returned to Armon.

"How was it over there?" he said.

"Very nice," she said.

There was a boy who Elyssa used to babysit who saw her and walked over to where they sat.

"Hi Elyssa," he said.

"Hi Leo."

"Why are you sitting over here?"

"We're not watching the movie. We're watching the people watch the movie."

The boy looked at Armon. Armon nodded.

"Do you want to sit and join us?" Elyssa said.

The boy watched with them.

"Nothing is happening," he said. But he didn't get up.

The boy's sister came over to check on him, with her friend behind her. This time Leo explained it. His sister and her friend sat and joined them.

"What if everybody comes over to this side?" Elyssa said.

"That's my dream," Armon said.

"That's your dream?"

"Yes."

"Who would we watch then?"

"Well, at that point, we wouldn't have to watch anybody. But if it came to it, I would go and sit over there so that they could watch me."

"You would? By yourself?"

"Yes."

"I would go with you," she said.

"That would be very nice."

There were young men who'd asked her to go places who didn't have the imagination for a place like that, and there was a young man who did but who hadn't thought of asking her there himself.

She wanted to tell him right there in front of Leo and Leo's sister and Leo's sister's friend that when two people could sit over there together, they already had the world watching, they had the whole world watching, even if they were the only two people in the park. She wanted to tell him they could have the whole world watching like that wherever they went. And even if they came to an outdoor movie in the park in the summer, they would have the whole world watching them while they sat among the crowd.

"Do you trust them?' she said.

"Who?"

"The people."

"I trust them from over here," he said. "I trust them unconditionally from over here."

"What does unconditionally mean?" Leo said.

"It means love," Armon said.

"I love them from here too," Leo said.

"See? Listen to Leo, he agrees with me."

"Yes," Leo said. "Listen to me."

Okay, she thought, so it started young. Amidst the crowd they felt lost and away from them, they loved them again. But what stayed the same? What stayed the same no matter where they were?

"Did you ever come to watch the movie?" she said.

"Yes," Armon said. "I did that last summer."

"Did you see anything good?"

"Yes, I think so. I can't remember it very well. I remember the crowds though."

"You do?"

"Yes. I figure I must remember them because I had dreams about them."

"What kind of dreams?"

"Nothing very exciting really. Just the people. Their faces. Same as this right now. They're boring dreams on the face of it, but the *feeling* of the dreams is a nice feeling."

"Is that why you started watching the crowds?"

"Yes. If your dreams are boring, it could mean you're a boring dreamer or it could mean life is wonderful. I am hoping it is the second one."

He was right, she thought. The rest of the time *was* far away. It was far away if they paid attention to the moment in front of them. He was trying to turn that attention into something, into something beautiful if he could. It was only natural that he was going to be far away sometimes himself in order to do that. Don't try to bring him back, she thought. Don't try to be a bridge. Just believe him when he says that if your dreams are boring, it could mean life is wonderful, and give your dreams a chance to be boring. They've had a long time to be exciting, but give them a chance to be boring and see how it goes.

THE REMINDER

You can be a good man on the court. That was what they didn't realize when they yelled at him for going to the rec center at night. They thought he was going to get away from everybody, from Mina and her mother and father and sister and from his own little boy, but it was because they didn't know the *way* he could be a good man there. You could take the principles you wanted to start the game with and you could put them into practice in actuality, and even exceed them, with new principles that could only be discovered in the flow of the game. It wasn't like that anywhere else. You could wake up in the morning and say, today I am going to find a steady job *and* go back to finish those classes at City College and be a good father to my boy and be a good husband to my wife, but none of it meant you had any say, none of it meant the world was working with you, however sure you were in what you had to say. But on the court, it was different, and you could tell yourself at the beginning of the game—Play hard, look for your teammates, be active on defense, move without the ball, and the words meant something. They added up to something you could point to and say, that is me. That is the man I am intending to be. It could be a help move on defense or an extra pass on offense. The world didn't give me a chance to be that man today, he wanted to tell them. But instead, he just left when they began to yell, and it made it look like the whole thing was a destructive act, and it wasn't until he stepped on the court that he remembered it wasn't. It was an act of creation. He couldn't explain it to them, but it was.

If only they could see him play, he thought. They would know.

Mina had seen him play years ago, but that was back when he stepped on the court thinking of himself. He had thought of what he wanted from the game, not of what the game wanted from him. He hadn't adhered to principles. He had been relying on hopes and wishes for the game. That wasn't who he was anymore. He could stay home at night with them and watch television programs that were a kind of hoping and wishing. But he wanted his son to know his father was going out to say something to the world at night. And he was saying something of his own choosing. The boy would see it, if Mina would let him bring him. She said he had to get his sleep, but then sometimes when he came home, the boy would be still lying awake, too excited or scared from the television program.

He would tell them all to come, the whole family. Look at this place, he thought. Look at the effort. Where else are they trying like this? Nowhere. Nowhere he saw in the day. But he would've tried like this in the day if there was a place for it. He would've moved without the ball and he would've helped on defense. And he would've been unselfish. That was a big part of it. They didn't give you a single place out there to be unselfish––they told you that you were being a sucker if you even considered it. They tried to tell you it wasn't natural, when he knew in his heart it was otherwise. It *was* natural. He knew it on the court because of how it felt. Nobody said you were being a sucker if you were unselfish there. He felt peaceful knowing that part of the game, and knowing it would outlast any aspects of running and jumping. That was the part that touched who *he* had been as a boy, and he knew then that everything they tried to tell him about how that boy was gone from who he was, was a lie. They tried to tell him he was a father now. You don't think I need that boy to be a good father? You don't think he was the best of who I ever was?

He felt himself touching the boy he was all during the game, with passes that came from somewhere he didn't know himself, with sequences where he saw what was about to happen in his mind just before it happened in life, with moments when he knew what was happening in another man's mind better than the man knew it himself. It was an invisible game sometimes. It was an invisible game, because nobody could see where the game you were playing came from. And it was so much like childhood because you could live in that mystery and nobody could tell you that you had to come out. You could build something in there. What they saw was the *results* of it. That was all they needed to see. Because the mystery filled you up as if it were food, the best food, grown from the earth and cooked slowly over time. *You think I could play like this if I didn't love my son? If I didn't love Mina, and her mother and father and sister as well? Of course I couldn't. You think I could see a man moving toward the basket like that if the day hadn't been made of love?*

During the game, it seemed effortless: He could greet their yelling with gentleness, the same gentleness that was needed for the soft parts of the game. If he could remember the game was made of the softest parts of himself and the hardest parts of himself, if he could remember it all the time, then he would have something. But at home, it was a vague memory, and he went with silence instead because it seemed like it was halfway between those two. Halfway was a long way from both though.

Remember this, he thought as he came back down the court on

defense. Remember your reach, remember your ability to affect the movements of others in a positive way. Remember your attunedness, your understanding of the present moment. Remember your humility, in not knowing more than you know.

The truths fit his body and his body fit the truths. They were the same thing. It was the only time they were the same thing. He could make his body fit a truth that supported his family, he would be willing to do that if given a chance. But nothing fit like this.

And for all that, the self still disappeared, until he *became* the game. He became a part of the eternal aspect of the game, going past his town and the night. He understood his present and his past. It had gotten him here. That was all that mattered.

His team won two of the three games. It was good to win, but it was better to play. Did anybody believe him when he said that? Would anybody believe him tonight when he came home and told them that tomorrow morning he would look for a job, but whatever happened, they shouldn't let it affect the belief in their *participation* in life.

After the game, the men who had jobs were quiet, thinking of how they were going to arise in their bodies tomorrow morning, wondering how much longer they would be able to ask their bodies to do both--the work they had to do and the game they loved. The men like him who did not have jobs, talked. They talked of the moments in the game, the ones when they had exceeded themselves, the ones they wanted to keep alive all the way home and possibly all the way through the night. Of the men who did not have jobs he was the only one who did not talk. You couldn't hold this thing in your hand, he thought. You couldn't slip it into your wallet and bring it home for everyone to see. No matter how well you played, it still wasn't money. He smiled. It was funny to still be surprised by that.

He could talk about the game with the rest of the men without jobs, but it wasn't the best way to hold on to what had just happened. Keep moving, was the best way. With the same grace that was there during the game. With the same quietness of purpose. As if there were no end to the game. As if Yancy didn't come into the gym at nine o'clock and tell them to clear out because he wanted to hurry up and get home. Some of the men gave him grief because it was better to talk in the light of the gym than outside in the parking lot. But it was best to keep moving, quietly, without much commotion, so as not to disturb the sense that you were a better man leaving the gym than you were coming in. Which you were. You had been a good man on the court, and you had seen that it was its own reward. You might be coming home empty-handed, without the money your family needed. But you weren't coming home to fight. He had seen the unnecessariness of that fight, just as he knew he would. And as he drove home, he knew the unnecessariness of that fight was not the same as the necessity of peace, that the dream of the family coming to see him play was perhaps foolish. But he would go home and have *something* he could give them. He could give them the reminder that the hardest parts of himself and the softest parts of himself were the same thing. He smiled again. It *was* a reminder because they all knew it themselves. It would be a reminder for all of them except the boy, who'd never forgotten it, and he hoped the boy would still be awake, too scared or excited from the television program, so that he could see that knowledge on his face himself.

ALL IS LOST

One day when he didn't expect it at all, the friendship between Katie Halverson and Allie Yarborough, which had been a constant in the life of Devin Basmajian in third grade and fourth grade and fifth grade and sixth grade, took on a sudden and great importance for him due to the possibility that it might be coming to an end, so much so that when he happened to notice Allie walk past Katie at the end of the day without saying hello, something went through his head that said, all is lost, and he decided he would not walk with the other boys to Dunnam Park to try to scare up a football game against the Etterman kids, and go home instead.

If Katie and Allie were no longer friends, then it was really true that something was changing in their lives, in all their lives, and Devin thought of all the times he had looked at Katie Halverson this year and liked her for how she stayed a girl and all the times he had looked at Allie Yarborough and liked her for how she was becoming a woman, and he felt how there was something certain and connected in his life as long as the two of them were friends, because a girl could still be a woman and a woman could still be a girl, and he had never guessed there could be a struggle inside their friendship. A struggle that said a girl could *not* be a woman and a woman could *not* be a girl, and that whatever each of them did from here on out, it would have to be on their own. He had never guessed that this thing that was changing in all their lives could carry something as destructive in it as that.

There were the days this year when Katie still wore overalls, he thought as he walked down Bay Hill Road by himself. Overalls and

121

her Stan Smith tennis shoes, and Allie wore a brown skirt that sent her legs straight to his heart, and yet the two of them would walk through the hall together full of things to tell each other, and when they did, he would see them and think that a man could be a man and still be a boy. That he did not have to draw a line in himself, even as everything in the world of boys and men had decided long ago there had to be a line, and that a boy had to either draw that line on himself or have it drawn on him by outside forces, which could be anywhere and could spring upon him in any number of unexpected ways. But as long as Katie and Allie were friends, there could still be both, there could still be both in them and there could still be both in him.

It was supposed to be *nice*, he thought. This thing that was changing in all their lives. He had already accepted it wasn't nice among boys, but if it wasn't nice among girls, if a girl who wore overalls and a girl who wore skirts could not stay as friends in seventh grade, then he didn't know how in the world anybody expected it to be nice *between* boys and girls.

The clouds were contending with the blue sky and the blue sky was winning as he walked home, but Devin still felt as though all was lost, and he felt then that he wished he could speak with Simon, his father's young cousin, who had come to see them last month and had spoken with his father about his divorce. Devin had wanted to play basketball with Simon and he kept dribbling past the window while they were talking, hoping that Simon would come outside. He had been a fool then and he had not known all was lost. He had not known that Katie Halverson and Allie Yarborough would not stay as friends in seventh grade, but if he had, he would have gone inside when Simon and his father were talking, and he would have listened and nodded in understanding about this thing that was clearly bound to end in defeat, as demonstrated by Simon's lost expression after only three years of marriage. Though it was true that Devin's own mother and father still danced in the kitchen sometimes.

But what *about* third grade and fourth grade and fifth grade and sixth grade? Did this new thing mean that all that stuff back there didn't matter? Did it have to be a struggle, a struggle to either hold on to that time or to cut it out completely? That meant there had to be a struggle either way, and he thought again that it was one thing if it was a struggle among boys, but if it was a struggle among girls, then it meant that whatever a boy and a girl could be together, they were both the veterans of a struggle. They were both limping their way to what they could be. They were, perhaps, not quite as much veterans of a struggle as Simon was when he had come to see them and he had that tired, lost face, but it was essentially close to the same thing.

That night at dinner he asked his father if Simon was going to visit them again soon.

"I don't know," his father said.

Devin sighed gravely.

"I know that you didn't get a chance to play basketball with him this time."

"It is not that."

"What is it then?"

"Well, I can't say it's a surprise."

"What?"

"His divorce," Devin said.

His father looked at his mother.

"Did you see it coming?"

"Yes," Devin said, because now it seemed that he had. It seemed now as though he'd always known that the friendship between Katie Halverson and Allie Yarborough could not survive, and if two girls could not bring their elementary school days with them, how could two adults hope to bring along the days that would help *them*?

"Perhaps you should have said something sooner," his father said.

"I would have," Devin said, "but everyone is always happy when two people get married."

"You did not want to be the voice of gloom and doom."

"No."

"I understand."

"Anyway, it is better if the people *try*."

"Of course."

"I'm not saying it's anybody's *fault*."

"No?"

"No."

It was too sad that Katie Halverson's and Allie Yarborough's friendship was ending for it to be anybody's fault. Katie wanted to be a kid for longer than Allie did and he understood that, and Allie wanted to be a woman sooner than Katie did and he understood that, too. There was nobody to blame. It just meant that if he eventually fell in love with either one of them, he would know what had gotten broken on the way there.

He watched them at school in the following days, and it was all true: Allie did not play handball with Katie or the other girls in their class. She sat with the eighth-graders in the yard who talked with great womanly understanding of all the secrets in everyone's hearts. Devin played basketball and even after making a beautiful pass to Mike Darling, he looked over and saw the two girls on opposite corners of the yard, and his heart fell. Their friendship simply could not hold. All those times out here in this same yard, jumping rope and comparing their eraser collections, but it was not enough. And he was lost in the sadness of it when Teddy Meadows's pass bounced off his hands and everyone laughed and told him to wake up. He couldn't hate them either; it was nobody's fault.

Walking home through Dunnam Park that afternoon, Cole Fangio asked Devin and Mike Darling who they liked, and Mike said Rebecca Kyle and Devin looked Cole in the eye and knew how much Cole loved for another boy to break when he said a thing like that, how much he loved to make it look like it was hard for everyone else so it must be easy for him, but he looked Cole in the eye and said, "Nobody," and Cole didn't say a word.

"You really don't like anybody?" Mike said later, when it was just the two of them walking.

"No."

"I told you who *I* liked."

"It's no use liking anybody."

"Why?"

He didn't think he could explain it to Mike. There were a lot of things he *could* tell him, but he didn't think he could tell him this one. *I like the* friendship *between Katie Halverson and Allie Yarborough. I like* that. *You know any way for me to like that once it's gone? You want me to explain that to a guy like Cole Fangio? A guy like him who doesn't think that third grade and fourth grade and fifth grade and sixth grade have anything to do with who you like?* If it were just that there were boys like him who didn't think that the old days had anything to do with liking anybody, that would be one thing, but if there were boys *and* girls who thought that, then this thing was no use, because how then were you supposed to like *all* of who somebody was?

"Ah, forget it," Devin said. They said goodbye when they got to Mike's street, and Devin felt bad for not explaining it to Mike, because he and Mike had been friends for even longer than Katie and Allie had, and if this thing that was happening now meant that *everybody* was going to leave aside the old days as though they hadn't mattered at all, then the whole thing was doomed, and he could almost understand becoming a guy like Cole Fangio, because he talked like he didn't care that the whole thing was doomed.

Devin tried to dream as he walked of Katie and Allie being friends again, dreaming his heart back into wholeness, and in the darkening afternoon he wondered for the first time if there was anything *he* had done himself in the effort to be one of the boys the girls noticed, maybe not as dramatic as Katie and Allie no longer talking, but if there was anything that had interrupted the wholeness of who *he* was, and he thought right away of Noah Parmalee across the street, even though a voice inside him said, come on, that's not the same thing at all, Noah is two years younger than you, still in elementary school. But Devin remembered very clearly now that when he'd decided to stop hanging around with Noah last summer, it was because he'd thought that if any girls from his class ever rode down his street, it wouldn't be good if they saw him hanging around with Noah. No girls ever rode down his street.

So, he thought, this is in me, too. Well, well, well. He had never felt so guilty and wise at the same time.

It was a heavy-hearted man who walked home that afternoon, and he wondered if it was better to like a girl like Allie Yarborough, who had been reckless in the pursuit of romance as he had, if it was better to seek a kind of commiseration together, or if he should like a girl like Katie Halverson, and throw himself towards redemption with a girl who still wore overalls and tennis shoes, and who certainly wouldn't care if she saw him hanging around with a fifth-grader like Noah Parmalee. It was a hell of a question. The streets and houses took on a darkness in the afternoon, and he understood why men in movies stopped in bars on the way home like the ones down along Fairhaven Street. There was something about being out in the world when you had a question like that inside you, like the full weight of it couldn't hit you if you didn't go home, and you could fight with the question as long as you stayed moving. He wanted to tell *somebody* what it was like to watch the friendship of two girls you knew over the years, from the time they were little. He would tell them about all the times he had gone out in the yard and seen the two of them on the monkey bars, sometimes just sitting up there together and talking. You don't know how much you like a thing like that while it's happening. You think they're just going to keep sitting up there and talking forever, but they're not.

Alright, he thought, when he had sunk about as low as he could go, this whole thing is doomed, but I can still do something. And he felt glad then he didn't have a place like a bar to go to, because it was better to do something than to feel sorry for himself, no matter how dark and wise a guy could look feeling sorry for himself in a bar.

He went straight to Noah Parmalee's house before going home.

Noah answered the door.

"Hi Noah."

"Hi."

"If you want to come outside later today, I'll come outside, too."
They had never had to arrange their hanging around outside before.

"It's going to rain."

Devin looked up at the sky. It *was* going to rain.

"Do you want to come outside now?"

"No. Do you want to play FIFA?"

Devin hated to play FIFA with Noah because he got angry when he lost.

"Alright. Let me put my backpack away."

"Okay."

Devin crossed the street to his house and he knew he'd either have to let Noah win or watch him get angry when he lost, and he laughed at the foolishness of everything, and in his laughter, he heard how all was not lost. *Most* was still lost, but most seemed like it had always been lost, even before Katie Halverson's and Allie Yarborough's friendship had come to an end. And the truth was, he felt okay about that, because most being lost somehow seemed to go with liking either one of them. He was sure they would each agree with him that most was lost, since their friendship was the perfect example, and if they could *start* from there, then he could build from what was left with either girl, no matter how small it was. He ran in and then ran back to Noah's house, and it felt very good to have things figured out.

WORTH IT TO BE WRONG

They were walking back from a football game. Winter was cold and gray, but it had been cold and gray for months in Seattle, so there were varieties, and today the air was clean almost enough to qualify for a clear sky.

They were a white couple. They were both twenty years old.

They walked to the edge of the campus, where the crowd changed from football fans to people out on a Saturday afternoon.

At the crosswalk, there was a young woman whose eyes were black and blue.

"I hate to see that," Abby said.

Tom looked at the woman and studied her.

"She was beaten," Abby said.

When they crossed the street, Tom said, "I don't think I would've known that if I were by myself."

She squeezed his arm. This is part of who we are, she thought.

They went to Tom's house.

"I am tired," Abby said. "Do you want to take a nap?"

"You don't know *for sure* though, that's how she got hurt."

She looked at him.

"I mean, if she got hurt in some other way, then you've wasted your concern."

"I have not wasted anything."

"I mean, everybody has stories. We can only be concerned with the ones we know for sure."

"Her face was not a story."

"Her face *was* a story. How can you say it was not a story?"

"Did you see her expression? She did not want to be out today."

"Maybe it was because she did not want people to have stories."

"You are the one who has a story."

"I don't have a story. I am saying I don't know what happened."

"Your story is she got hurt by something other than a man."

"It might've been that. But I don't know for sure."

"If you really thought she might've been hurt by a man, you would not have a calm and logical place to hold that thought."

"There is nothing wrong with logic."

"There is something wrong with logic if a woman has to prove she was beaten when she looks like that."

"You don't know it for sure."

This is also part of who we are, Abby thought. He climbs up somewhere high and then he gets scared.

"How do you think she got hurt?"

"I don't know."

"You believed me in the street."

"I didn't have a chance to think about it."

"What did you realize when you thought about it?"

"I realized it was *possible* she got hurt in some other way. And if she did, we would have felt bad for nothing."

"It wouldn't have been for nothing."

"Yes, it would have. Of course it would have. It's exhausting to go around thinking you know everything about people."

"It seems more exhausting to me to fight what you know."

"I am not fighting anything. That is my whole point."

"What is your whole point?"

"My whole point is, I am walking down the street with you.

I am holding hands with you and walking home. And at that moment, you want me to hate another man, too. You want me to hate him enough to fight him."

"You did for a moment."

"Yes. But we kept walking and we came home and you asked me if I wanted to take a nap with you, didn't you?"

Abby did not know what to say.

"If it's a fight, then it should be a fight," Tom said. "You can't give me these fights and then take them away. What am I supposed to do with them?"

"Do you want me to not say anything?"

"I want you to have a *reason* to tell me things like that."

"You know the reason."

"What is the reason?"

"I do not want to say it. If I have to say it, I am going to want to leave."

"I think you should say it."

"You don't care if I leave?"

"I don't want you to leave. But I think it will be better in the long run if you say it. What is going to happen in the future if you say things and I don't know the reason?"

"The reason is love. I thought the reason was love."

"What am I supposed to do with that?"

"I am going to leave."

"You are telling me something you hate, and something I hate, and you are saying the reason is love."

"I did not tell anything. The woman was there."

"You did tell something. You said she was beaten."

WORTH IT TO BE WRONG

"She *was* beaten!"

"How do you know? How do you know for sure?"

"I am going to go home."

"Just answer it. That's all I'm asking you."

"You are talking like a lawyer. You are my boyfriend."

"I'm trying to help."

"How? How are you trying to help?"

"I'm trying to help because if you don't have to feel bad, then you shouldn't. If you don't know for sure, then you're ignoring the chance you could be wrong."

"It's worth it for me to be wrong."

"Well, I don't feel that way. It's never worth it for me to be wrong."

"It's worth it for me because it happens all over the place."

"That doesn't mean it happened with her."

"But it shouldn't even cross my mind. It shouldn't even be one of the possibilities."

"You have a choice about what crosses your mind."

"No. I don't. We don't see the world in the same way if you think I have a choice about what crosses my mind."

"You can look at her and say, maybe that's what happened, and maybe it was something else."

"Where do you go from there?"

"The same place you go with most people. You don't know their stories, so all you can do is focus on your own."

"It did not feel like a maybe."

"Of course it didn't feel like a maybe. But it was a maybe. It has to be maybe, or else—"

"Or else what?"

"Or else, there are no limits to anything. What's to stop you from wondering about everybody?"

"I didn't say I was wondering about her."

"But you were. There is either knowing or wondering."

"Alright. Then I know she was beaten."

"But you don't."

"I say that I do. You don't have to agree with me."

"How can you expect me to agree with you?"

"You don't have to."

"You're going to go home if I don't agree with you, aren't you?"

"I want to go home either way."

"I'm sorry. Let's take a nap."

"I'm not tired. There is a side to take when you see a woman like that."

"There are too many sides to take. That's all I would be doing, is taking sides, if I start doing that."

"I think they are all the same side."

She left. It had been cloudy and gray in Seattle for so long and the air was so clean that it was a while before she remembered it was not a sunny day.

PROVERBS

Taraneh asked her mother and when her mother did not know, she asked her father and when her father did not know, the adventure started.

"I will call my cousin," her father said. "I will ask him."

Her father called his cousin at the gas station where he worked.

"Massoud jaan," her father said. "The apple doesn't fall far from the tree. It is Taraneh's homework."

"Is it a math problem?" Massoud said.

"Is it a math problem?" her father said.

"No," Taraneh said. "It is a proverb. I have to say what it means."

"It is a proverb," her father said.

"Of course the apple doesn't fall far from the tree," Massoud said.

"Where else is it going to go?" her father said, laughing.

"Unless the tree is on a hill."

"Ah."

"But that would be poor planning."

"Do you remember when we would steal cucumbers from the Ghaffaris' farm?"

"Those were the best cucumbers I've ever had."

"Have you seen at the supermarkets here they sell *Persian* cucumbers?"

"Yes. They are not as good as Persian cucumbers."

"When do you go to the supermarket?" Taraneh's mother said.

"I read the package when you bring them home."

"If a customer comes in, I will ask them about this apple," Massoud said.

"Baba, there is another one," Taraneh said.

"Massoud jaan, there is another one."

"A bird in the hand is worth two in the bush."

"A bird in the hand is worth two of them in the bush."

"A bird?"

"Yes."

"What kind of bird?"

"It does not say."

"It must be small to fit in a hand."

"Yes."

"There are a lot of bushes and trees in these proverbs."

"Yes. You would think they would keep more nature around instead of these endless freeways."

"Maybe that is where nature survives, in their proverbs."

"Ah, that is beautiful. Taraneh, you should write a composition about how there is more nature in these proverbs than in the society itself."

"That is not the assignment."

"That is too bad."

"I will give you the phone number of my friend," Massoud said. "He is a Kurd. He has been here for ten years. He will know."

Taraneh's father switched to Turkish to speak to the Kurd. He explained the situation. "Agha Kamal, suppose you have an apple. Suppose this apple does not fall far from the tree. What do you conclude from that?"

"I have the apple before it falls?"

"No, the apple has fallen. You are walking by and you see that it is not far from the tree."

"It does not say anything about walking by," Taraneh's mother said.

Taraneh listened and did not understand her parents speaking in Turkish, but she felt proud her father would call up a man he did not know. She felt proud of the Kurd, too, because she could tell that he was trying.

"*Somebody* has to see the apple," Taraneh's father said to her mother. "What do you think he is doing if he is not walking by?"

"Just say it as it is written."

Her father said it as it was written.

Agha Kamal was silent over the phone.

"It means you cannot trust anybody," he said. "That is why the apple stays close to the tree."

"Thank you. Are you sure?"

"No. But that is how I feel here."

"You miss your country?"

"Yes. Do you miss Iran?"

"Yes."

"At least you have a country. That is good."

"I have always felt your people deserve their own country."

"Thank you. I don't think I will see it."

"I hope you will see it."

Taraneh's father said goodbye and hung up the phone.

"Did you ask him about the second one?" she said.

"No."

"Did he know about the first one?"

"No."

She looked at her mother, who looked away.

"Let's go and ask the neighbors," her father said. "Put your shoes on."

Taraneh felt excited to bring the neighbors into it. She and her father put their shoes on.

"Ask the left-side neighbors," her mother said. "You should take something. Take the box of chocolates."

"Maybe we should take some apples," her father said. He winked at his daughter.

"Let me find a bow first," her mother said.

"Maybe we can just trade them a proverb. One American proverb for one Iranian proverb."

"They don't want one of our proverbs."

"Of course they do. Everybody needs proverbs. I would rather have a proverb than chocolate."

Taraneh was about to say she would rather have chocolate, but her father looked too happy for her to say it.

"What would you tell them?" her mother said, as she looked for a bow.

"Whoever has a bigger roof has more snow on their roof."

"No. That is not a good one for a neighbor. They might take it personally."

"We have the same-sized roof!"

"And it doesn't snow here," Taraneh said.

"The sound of the drum is pleasant from a distance. I like that one," her mother said.

"What does it mean?" Taraneh said.

"It means there are a lot of things that seem wonderful when you are far away but they are not as good when you are up close."

"We really do have some good proverbs," her father said.

"Yes, but you should still take the box of chocolates."

"Okay. I hope they will like them as much as they would like a proverb."

Before they could go, the phone rang. It was Massoud. A customer had come in and he had asked him and Massoud had learned the whole story. Taraneh's father listened intently as he explained it.

"I see," he said.

"They are good proverbs," he said to his family after he hung up the phone. He explained them to his wife and his daughter, who listened just as intently as he had.

They were silent for a moment, each of them thinking in their own way of how they had left one place with proverbs and come to another place with proverbs.

"Should we still give them the chocolates?" Taraneh's father said.

They had been at this apartment for a year, the left-side neighbors for a few months. They had said some hellos to each other, so far.

"I think so," her mother said.

Taraneh and her father walked over to their place.

"This feels like we're in a proverb," she said.

Her father laughed. "That's just what I was thinking."

They rang the doorbell and introduced themselves and gave

them the box of chocolates. It was funny to welcome an American family to their new neighborhood in America. As they walked back, Taraneh thought of apples and birds in a bush and snow and the sound of drums, and she felt pretty sure she was going to make up all kinds of proverbs in her life, most likely in Farsi and English, both.

THE TROPHY

The thing about the guy was he was so calm when he came in. He took his time looking over the shelves. I figured maybe he was a little league coach. That's who I get the most. That's the good thing about being close to the park. They play over there and then when they need trophies, they come to my shop.

He picked up a little one, a two-handled cup, and brought it to the counter.

"You do engraving?"

"Yes, sir."

"Alright. I want it to say, 'You win, Everything is my fault.'"

That's when he broke, just as he said it. I could see he didn't mean it. But he tried to steady himself. "See how she likes *that*."

So that's how it is, I thought. I looked out the window. It was a pretty day, with the sun lingering out over the ocean.

"How long will it take?"

"You can pick it up tomorrow morning."

"I'll wait."

He went outside and took out a cigarette. I wanted to go outside and tell him something, like how I could see how he didn't mean it. But I wasn't used to talking to customers about a job. He sat on the curb and smoked. Hell, I thought, you don't know the guy's wife. Maybe she deserves the trophy.

I went to work. I centered "You win" and put "Everything is my fault below it." Nice block letters. I looked up and saw the guy walk around outside and smoke another cigarette. Somehow, I felt like whatever happened, I had to finish the job. But still, I worked slowly, thinking it would give him more time to reconsider. Maybe it's just a joke, I thought. But everything in his movements and his words suggested it was not a joke, that it was his final stab at having the last word, as though the trophy could just sit on their mantel somewhere and he'd be able to just point to it the next time a fight started up and not even have to say anything. I'd never felt so sad engraving a trophy before, like I wanted to throw it away when I was done with it.

The guy waited patiently outside and I couldn't tell if he was reconsidering, but I told him it was done and he came back in as eagerly as he'd started.

"There's one problem," I said. "I'm not going to sell it to you."

"What?"

"I like to finish a job. But I'm not going to sell it."

"I've been standing here for an hour—"

"I'm sorry about that. I'm sorry I didn't say it sooner. I didn't know it till I got done."

"What the hell is this?"

"Just what I said. I'm not going to sell it."

"Why the hell not?"

"This can't be it."

"Can't be what?"

"It can't be the thing you have to give her."

For just a moment he looked to me like a little boy.

"Do you know her?" he said.

"No."

"Then how do you know it's not the thing she needs?"

"Well," I said. "I think you haven't given up."

"The hell I haven't."

"Look," I said. "You could've written her a note. But you came in here and you thought you'd buy a trophy. The thing about trophies is, they are for *display*. Sure, the metal is cheap and some of 'em the gold wears off after a while. But people buy them because they like to have them out for everybody to see. If you're buying a trophy, you got something you want people to see, and that means there's still a *we*. People don't buy trophies to hide them away."

"Sure," he said. "I want it on display. I want everybody to see what she drove me to."

"Well, you're going to have to tell her yourself."

"You're not going to let me have it?"

"No."

"What the hell are you going to do with it?"

"I'm going to leave it up here as an example of the kind of trophies I don't sell. The kind of trophy that, if you're going to come in here and ask me to make, I'm going to tell you to go home and talk with your wife instead."

"Talk with her and tell her what?"

"Tell her the truth. Tell her you went to a trophy shop and the guy wouldn't sell you the trophy you wanted and told you to talk with her instead, and then talk."

"*Then* what?"

"Tell her how you felt while you were waiting for a trophy like that."

"Out there?"

"Yes."

"Dead. I felt dead."

"Alright. Ask her if she feels dead."

"What if she says no?"

"That's good. It means you haven't killed her."

"What if she says yes?"

"That's good. It means you can try to become alive together."

"Are you really going to keep the trophy?"

"Yes."

"People are going to think it's a joke."

"*Is* it a joke?"

"No. I don't think so. I don't know."

"It *is* funny."

"It's funny, but it's dead."

"Maybe it's not dead if I keep it. The people who see it will only think it's funny."

"Hell," he said. "You can tell them. You can tell them some dumb mope came in here and after seventeen years of marriage, this was the best he could do."

"It's not the best you can do."

"I don't know what else I got."

"You're leaving it here, aren't you? *That's* the best you can do."

"It's something, I guess."

He turned to go.

"Come by and look at it if you want," I said.

"No," he said. "Let the people laugh at it. It's not funny to me."

"Okay," I said. "I'll tell them to laugh in the right way about it."

"Thanks."

I wasn't sure exactly what that way was, and I didn't think the guy knew either, but I thought I would know it when I heard it.

GOOD TRY

The games were on Friday evenings. Last year, they played on Sundays, and that had been better, because on the weekends, Will Penny remembered that he was more than a kindergarten teacher. He remembered that there was a roughness and hardness in the life of men, and he could step on the field assured in that memory. But on Fridays he had to go straight from the school, and even though he would try to leave who he had been all week behind, he couldn't help it: when somebody on his team struck out or made an error, he would say, "Good try."

The men on his team were not men who dealt in good try. It hit them wrong. They were bartenders and chefs and mechanics, and one magazine writer who was an especially cynical one. They wanted to tell Will to shut up when he said good try, but they knew he was coming from childhood.

What was it that made a man no longer want to hear good try once he had seen a certain aspect of life? The men on the team could not remember a time when they would have been glad to be told good try. If they had been, they were better off not remembering that time. They had made some kind of peace with the way that good tries didn't have much to do with life. It had to do with a secret belief, possibly even secret from themselves, that *all* of childhood had been a good try, but where did it get you?

They could take some comfort in the way they all knew that together, but when Will would tell them good try, their collective grip on that knowledge would be shaky.

Will knew it himself. He knew he should leave good try at

the school and in the playground where he watched over games of handball and Steal the Bacon.

But it was hard. The grass at the field was like the grass at the school, and the sky in the evening was like the sky in the afternoon, so he felt like other things might be the same, too. When he said "good try," it really looked to him like a good try, like a good try in the game and like a good try in life.

Why can't a man be who he is among children, among men? Will Penny didn't know. He was saying good try to children with the understanding that the boys among them at least would grow up to *be* men. Good try had saved many kids from crying or getting upset when they got out or lost a game. He could understand if the men did not like that implication, but it still did not seem like a *bad* thing to say.

He was only trying to build up the people around him, same as he did all day.

Sometimes Will's voice rang out over the field and the players on the other team would notice the way he was trying to build up the people around him. The men on his team drank beer in many of the same bars as the other players in the league and they learned that their reputation around town had become that of the Good Try Team.

That did it. The men decided they had to have a talk with Will. They couldn't stomach the thought that people were beginning to see them and think of a good try.

Nobody wanted to say anything before the next game though. They *wanted* to tell him that good try had no place on a baseball field when the people doing the playing were men, but it was hard to present substantive evidence as to why. They didn't want him to start saying *bad* try. They realized what they were advocating was his silence, which made them wonder what was so important about silence among men. And they knew what it was—it was the sense that in his silence a man was going to the same place inside himself that was inside his fellow man, but it felt like it would break the whole thing open to verbalize it, in a way that would be irreparable. So, they stayed silent because as long as there was silence, there was a sense of that was the place they all went together.

Will's voice became even more prominent as the men became silent, and the opposing players wondered why only one guy on their team was doing all the talking.

Something made the men feel powerless in the face of good try. Part of them wondered if they had been told good try enough as boys. They could hear the building intention in Will's voice. It was a strange feeling to be believed-in like that. They wondered about the children who heard it every day from Will. They thought that maybe they became the confident men and women they saw sometimes in the city.

Of course, the other possibility was they *expected* to hear good try their whole lives and they never learned to stand on their own two feet. The men preferred to take this position.

The first time someone finally said "good try" to Will was in the sixth game of the season. It was Derek Willoughby. The men gave him an incriminating look.

"'Good try?'" Sean Gilligan said.

"Yes."

"He's been talking to kids. What's your excuse?"

"It was a good try."

Sean Gilligan spat disgustedly at a tree.

He hadn't known that in his mind he'd given Will Penny an excuse for saying good try.

What were they going to do, start saying good try left and right now? A man had to be on top of something. He couldn't always be climbing it. He had to be sitting on top of it sometimes, looking down.

That was the thing about good try, the men thought in their silence—when would you ever *stop* saying it once you started? Good try, world. Good try, life. Good try, everybody everywhere. There was no boundary to it.

Will Penny felt the same way on Friday afternoons. He felt there was no boundary to the way a man could build up a child's sense of who they were by seeing their effort, by letting them know their effort was a seen thing. The school grounds certainly did not seem like a boundary, not when everything else about life seemed the same.

He laughed when Sean Gilligan turned back to the game after Derek Willoughby said good try and called out to him, "Good try, Will! You almost ran it out, but no milk and cookies for us! We have to go have nap time, and then we can wake up and have show-and-tell!"

He laughed because he could hear how Sean Gilligan didn't mean it. Or that he didn't know what he meant. Or that the silence men went into instead of saying good try was a reasonable place to go, all things considered, which it was. Will Penny knew it was because he knew how much he needed a place to go to each day where he could say good try, as part of his own trying. He knew how important it was for men to have silence as the second-best option.

It was just that the games were on Fridays, and he couldn't help it.

"Okay," he called out to Sean Gilligan "but please raise your hand next time, or you'll have to sit in the time-out chair!"

Everybody burst out laughing. Sean Gilligan laughed, too. Okay, Will thought. I just hope you know I got this laughter from kids.

They made a kind of uneasy peace with being known as the Good Try Team that season. The next season the schedule put them back on Sundays, and Will would have had a couple of days for his week with kids to wear off him, and he would have his own silences to go into during the games, his own moments of wondering about who he was blending with thoughts of the game, blending with the necessary compromises with dreams and the gentle sadness of Sundays. At least for the first few games of the season, he would miss the way the men would throw a quick glance in his direction after getting out, looking to see if he would say the words that gave a beat they could fill in with the musicality of their own lives.

THE USE OF LANGUAGE

The world was getting slow for him, and so Hadi Samarkar decided to learn a new language. He'd learned that it was the thing. There was alcohol and women and gambling, but when he got like this, a new language was the thing.

It was when everybody seemed to be moving around lumberingly. There was no grace or style or nuance to their movements. He knew it wasn't the truth—there *was* grace and style and nuance there, because people were infinite, but he was not seeing it because he was not seeing them in a way that was new.

When he learned a language, he remembered a people. The people who had lived and died in that tongue. They had done everything human beings could do in it. Oh, he would think, that's right. The story of the people would come back to him, and in the process the story of himself would come back, too.

It had something to do with learning everything from scratch. You remembered what a table was when you learned the word for table. It was a hell of a thing. You took a little pride in human beings for coming up with the table. It was like being a kid, but he tried not to think about that directly. He was a fifty-five-year-old man learning a language, that's all.

He went to the Hudson Park branch of the New York Public Library and sat down with some books at a table. He always started with books. It was how he'd learned French, Spanish, Italian, and German. He'd learned Farsi, English, Turkish, and Arabic back in Iran.

The books were teaching Hungarian. He did not know the

first thing about Hungary. He liked it that way. He would let the language tell him about the people.

The third evening there, the librarian saw him and wondered why this man was coming in to learn Hungarian. Her head filled up with stories explaining it. She settled on a love story. There was a Hungarian woman he missed. He looked like he could be a man who missed somebody. She began to think of it each time she saw him.

One night an old man sat across from Hadi and saw what he was reading.

"You are learning my language," the old man said.

"You are Hungarian?"

"Yes."

They both smiled. There was some kind of recognition for both of them. Here was the old man this language was trying to describe, Hadi thought. It fit. The old man spoke the language and the language spoke the old man. Hadi felt very glad he had been learning it.

The librarian walked over to hear what they were saying. Both of the men *thought* she was walking over to hush them, and they went back to reading. The librarian wished the people who came to the library could know she was more than *just* a librarian.

When she went to the other side of the room, the old man whispered, "May I ask why it is that you are learning Hungarian?"

"I like languages."

"Do you like Hungarian?"

"Yes."

The old man felt proud. "What do you like about it?"

"Everything," Hadi said. "I can see the people."

"You can?"

"Yes."

The old man did not know what to think. He felt slightly defensive. It took more than sitting in a library in New York to see the people. At the same time, he felt how the language did contain the people, too. He trusted Hadi's vision a little more because he could see that he was also not American.

"Where are you from?" he said.

"Iran."

"Maybe someday I will learn your language."

"You're welcome to it."

The librarian saw them then and casually walked over to hear what they were saying. But they assumed she was coming to casually hush them. This was a part of her job nobody had told her about. People saw her as a warden practically. She had become a librarian because she loved books, not because she enjoyed hushing people.

She decided she would take a more direct route. The next time he came, she told Hadi about the conversational language program at the Kupferberg Institute.

"Maybe there is somebody for you to practice Hungarian with," she said.

"I hadn't thought of that," Hadi said.

"Do you already have somebody to practice with?"

"No," he said.

In her years at the library, she had seen all kinds of people with all kinds of interests. Nothing surprised her anymore. But a language was something you learned in order to speak it with someone. It would just be lonely to learn it and hold it by yourself.

"Well, you should look into the institute."

"Thank you."

Hadi came in most evenings over the next few weeks. He was getting better. He could understand simple sentences. He saw what the people of Hungary had been trying to do. They had been trying to live. They were not so different from him in that sense.

Maybe he would go there some day. He was a photographer, and his work had once taken him around the world. In Argentina, he had married a woman and brought her to New York. They'd had a son. When he was five, she had gone back to Argentina and taken the boy with her.

It was life. As he learned the Hungarian language, he felt like it wasn't unheard of. It wasn't so crazy that it couldn't be put into words. The language was ready for him. He felt glad to know there was a place where his story would not come as a surprise.

He knew it was true for the places whose languages he already spoke, but it was something about the *discovery* of it. It brought other discoveries along the way.

Little by little, he began to see it in the life around him in New York. People were alright. They were not as quick and lively as they could be, but they hadn't forgotten about quickness and liveliness. All a language could do was give them the words. They had to do the rest.

The librarian, whose name was Alice Denman, still wondered about Hadi. He didn't seem like the people who came in and asked her about things that made her feel sorry for them. You saw a lot as a librarian. You saw people's secret hearts, the thing they didn't show anybody out in the world. It gave her a different view of them out in the world. They acted like they had things figured out, like there weren't a million things they wanted to know. But she had never seen anybody wanting to learn a language they couldn't speak with anybody. That one confounded her. She didn't care about making stories anymore. She wanted to know.

There had to be *somebody* he was learning it for. She felt sorry for *herself* somehow when she thought of him sitting and learning Hungarian. Life was hard enough, Alice Denman thought, without a language inside you that couldn't come out.

So, one evening she asked him again if he had gone to the language institute.

"No," Hadi said. "I may still do it, though."

She suddenly frowned at him. "That's what these books are for, you know. For learning how to *speak* with other people."

She didn't know herself where her frown came from.

"They help me with speaking," Hadi said. "Just not in Hungarian."

He smiled at her.

This is what happened when people saw you as some kind of warden, Alice Denman thought.

"Don't you want to speak it with somebody?" she said.

"Someday," Hadi said.

He took the books and sat in his usual spot, same as where he'd sat and talked with the old Hungarian man. It was funny, he thought, that people thought the only thing about a language was its use, like saying the only point of reading Shakespeare was to perform it in a play. The language had everything—people and what they'd said and what they'd only ever said to themselves and even somehow, something unsayable, too. Something that stayed unsayable no matter how many languages a man learned.

THE CALENDAR

My father kept his heroes alive for me as long as he could. He told me later that he hadn't meant to do it, but the way I'd listened had made him do it. He told me about Martin Luther King, Malcolm X, Che Guevara. They were alive in his stories. I was little and I hadn't started elementary school yet. All I knew was what he told me, and how happy he was when he spoke about them. I couldn't wait till I was older and could be as happy about them as he was.

I started kindergarten when I was five. At the beginning of each month, our teacher, Ms. Meyer, would have one student come to the front of the class and mark the important dates on the calendar as she read them. In January, it was my turn. She gave me a sticker and announced that January 20th was Martin Luther King Day.

Before I even put on the sticker, I said, "Is he coming to our school?"

"No, Nina," Ms. Meyer said. "He isn't alive anymore."

I stood with the sticker and didn't do anything. I looked at the class. Nobody was surprised he wasn't alive anymore. People died, but I didn't know Martin Luther King had died.

When I came home that afternoon, I kept waiting for my father to come home from work. I was going to be mad at him. Ms. Meyer had used the nice voice she used for kids in our class who didn't know something they should know. I'd heard her use it on other kids, but I'd never heard her use it on me. It felt good to be mad at my father. He had told me a story, but he hadn't told me the *whole* story. I didn't know why he had done that. I didn't like the thought that he only wanted me to hear the part of the story that was alive.

When my father came home, I didn't hug him like I usually did.

"Martin Luther King is dead!" I said.

"Nina!" my mother said.

"Yes," my father said. He looked very sad. "He is."

It was hard to be mad at my father when he looked so sad, but I had been waiting for a long time.

"Ms. Meyer told me!" I said.

"Nina, that's not the way to say hello to your father!" my mother said.

My father took a deep breath and sat down. He put his head in his hands. "I'm sorry," he said. "You're right. He's dead. I'm sorry." He stayed sitting there with his head in his hands longer than I could stay mad at him, and longer than my mother could stay mad at me for not running and saying hello to him and hugging him the way I usually did.

THE SPEAKER'S APPRENTICE

After college, Shayan Ghorbanian worked in a hotel. He wrote letters about the place to a girl in Texas. He hadn't set out to write about the place. He had set out to write love letters. But it seemed like the best way to do it once he started was to show her the place where he thought of her.

He wrote to her about the football fan club that had come for a banquet and about the religious group whose members spoke in tongues.

"There's all kinds of people in the world, Lucy," he wrote. "And I like you."

She was a friend of his cousin's and they had kissed at a party.

One day there was a talk in the main ballroom by a motivational speaker. Shayan listened as he arranged water pitchers in the back of the room. He was already thinking of Lucy and of writing the letter in his head.

I don't know, he thought. The people don't *look* unmotivated. They were certainly motivated enough to come here early in the morning and take notes and listen closely. Me, I'd like to listen to someone who didn't look so polished. There's a difference between being polished and confident. I don't know what it is yet. But maybe a really confident guy would get on stage and say, Beats me. What do you guys think? I don't know how well that would go over. I'd pay to see a guy like that. That might actually be fun. For all the different groups I've seen in this place, I can't shake the notion that there *can* be something nice about a group of people together in a big room. I haven't seen it yet, but I think it can be. It always *looks* like it can be to me, right up until the start of the event. That's why I like to come in and watch everybody during the breaks. The whole thing doesn't look so bad then.

He was too busy writing the letter to notice the fellow next to him saying hello.

"Hi buddy."

Shayan looked to see that it was the speaker's apprentice. There were two of them. They weren't assistants because they did everything the speaker did, just on a smaller scale.

"Can I ask you a question?"

"Okay."

"Would you like to be retired at thirty?"

"Retired at thirty?"

"Yes!"

"That seems like a very young age to retire."

The apprentice got very excited. "Why not? Why not shoot for something like that?"

"Well, to answer your question, I don't want to be retired at thirty."

"You don't?"

"No."

The apprentice looked at Shayan as though this were the first time somebody had ever said no.

"I'd like to be doing *something*," Shayan said.

"You could do whatever you wanted if you were retired."

"What I mean is, I don't dream of retirement."

Shayan thought then that the apprentice would walk away. It seemed like non-retirement dreams were past his apprenticeship.

"What do you dream of then?"

"Well, there's a girl. She is in Texas though. Also, I dream of how it would be if everybody had to work in a hotel, at least for a little while."

He laughed. "That would never happen."

"Aren't you not supposed to say that?"

He smiled. "You have to be realistic."

"Well, you wanted to know what I dream of. That's one thing. It's not bad working in a hotel. I've seen a lot of interesting things. I just think that if everybody had to spend a little while in their life working in a hotel, it would be a different thing. Everybody would come in and say, hey, hey, there's the old lobby just like the one I used to pass through. And of course, they'd look at the people there a lot differently. They wouldn't just pass by them, because they would know that used to be them. So, they'd stop and chat for a few minutes. And the manager wouldn't yell at them, because they'd be busy catching up with all the old managers passing through."

"Nothing would get done," the apprentice said.

"Well, I grant you things would move more slowly. But that would be alright. The events could overlap anyway if everybody had something in common. The people in the football fan club could let in the people who speak in tongues. Maybe they could all hear some motivational speaking."

"The way you're describing it, it doesn't sound like they're going to need it."

"Well it can't hurt. They're all going to be there in the room anyway."

The speaker wrapped up, and gave a quick look to both

apprentices on either side of the room.

"Good luck," Shayan said.

"Thank you," the apprentice said.

The next day Shayan was putting out the morning coffee when he saw that only the speaker and the other apprentice had come down to the ballroom.

"Where's your buddy?" Shayan said to the other apprentice.

"Mike?" the fellow said.

"Yes."

"He's staying back today."

"What happened?"

"This is a tough business. Tougher than I had thought."

"What happened?"

"He said something he wasn't supposed to say."

Shayan had a sick feeling. He looked at the speaker, arranging his notes at the podium. He looked like he hadn't said, Beats me. What do you guys think? in a very long time.

"What did he say?" Shayan said.

The fellow looked at him. He looked for an angle and saw none.

"He said 'how come we don't ever motivate people to do anything together.'"

Shayan smiled. He thought of Lucy at the party. She had looked so beautiful. Of the three letters he had written her, she had replied to none. He had a good feeling about this one. Not so much that she would write back necessarily, but that one way or another, he would know where he stood after this one.

THE MYTH

He told her it was funny she should say that, because there was actually a myth, a famous unknown legend, about people who had a low tolerance when it came to alcohol. What it was was that it wasn't that they had a low tolerance, it was that they had something *already*. They had something that was ready for whatever it was that took most people five or six drinks to achieve, and they had that readiness because of a kind of churning going on inside them all the time, a churning that took in people and time and dreams and love, not just the love that was right there in front of them, but all of it, even the love that existed in hate, that knew at the bottom of hate *was* love, and the bottom line was any *decent* society would actually have *more* respect for the people who became drunk after one drink. It wouldn't laugh at them or make fun of them, it would respect them for moving through their day in a way that was only one drink away from drunkenness, because it was hard work moving through a day like that. You had to work hard to see a great many things that most people didn't see, including the sun and the sky and the movement of people. You had to *work*, that was the point of it, and your body knew you deserved to be drunk after one drink even if you didn't know it yourself, even if you laughed about it or made fun of it *yourself*. They were special, the ones who could get drunk after one drink, and the real truth of it was they were misnamed in being said to have a low tolerance. The real truth of it was they had a *high* tolerance—they had a high tolerance for life and everything it gave them, and they didn't build walls to say life could give them this but it couldn't give them that, they took in the whole thing, so they just had more to mix in with that first drink than most people did, only they had to play it cool and act like it was no big deal while everybody else drank through the night, so that was another thing they had a high tolerance for—patience, the patience it took for everybody to catch up to where they already were—teetering between hope and despair, between comedy and tragedy, between joy and sorrow.

"But it was funny," he said, wrapping up the myth—"it was funny how much those people discovered teetering didn't feel like teetering when you had been teetering all day. And what a strong and sure thing it could be."

SO LONG

When I first heard it, I thought maybe somebody was messing with him. I thought somebody had said to him, Here's how you can sound more American, and then given him something straight out of the 1930's. It made me mad. Mahmoud's was the only corner store in the neighborhood run by an Iranian, and I used to go out of my way to stop in there when I needed something and to say hello. "Hello buddy," he would say when he saw me, which was natural enough, but it was what he said when I left, which was: "So long."

So long. I didn't hear anybody else saying that all day long. And I was a listener to language. I was trying to learn to write in a way that would knock the one-and-a-half years of creative writing classes I'd taken out of me. No offense to those classes, I just wanted to write differently from how they were doing it there.

I wanted to write like people still had stories. Not just things they could say, but things they really *wanted* to say. Like everybody was the kind of person you'd like to be sitting with on Friday night around nine o'clock at one of the round tables at a good bar like Specs. Because they were. That's how I felt when I walked out of the class in the evening. That was exactly who they were. I just didn't know how I was going to prove it.

Anyway, I used to listen to conversations a lot in those days, and it made me happy almost to the point of seriousness that the only person I heard saying something as beautiful-sounding as So long was a fellow countryman. If somebody had been trying to mess with him, they didn't know what Iranians could do with language. They could take anything wistful or heartfelt and multiply it by a factor of ten. When I was a kid my father used to break my heart and send me soaring at once by the way he would say when he dropped me off at school, "Have fun."

I wanted to ask Mahmoud Agha about it, but I didn't want to say something that would make him start thinking about everything he said. It wasn't as though anybody thought twice about it when he said it. I'd heard him say So long to Americans and they didn't bat an eye, even though he stretched out the word *so* in such a way that the whole thing could never in good faith be written like this the way he said it: s'long. But that didn't change its miraculousness for me.

The thing that was so wonderful when he said it, was that I felt like we Iranians had been in America longer than we actually had. I felt like we had a real history here, going back to before the revolution, before the 1953 coup d'etat, back to a time when—in my imagination at least—people were expected to have stories, because they were expected to provide a larger percentage of a night's entertainment for each other. Which is not to say Iranians would've had it easy in America back then if any of us *had* been around. It was just a nice thing to imagine for a little while.

You've got to give yourself something to feel a little secure in your foothold when you're new to a country, and for me it was when I heard Mahmoud Agha say So long.

There were some days his wife would be at the front counter while Mahmoud Agha put away new inventory in the back.

"How long have you been in America?" I asked her once in Farsi.

"Eight years," she said. "How long is it for you?"

"We came when I was four. I'm twenty-five."

"So, you are American."

"I suppose."

I didn't mind her saying it, because I certainly *felt* American when I sat at my desk to write. I wanted to write in a way that was an extension of the street outside, and the street was an American street, so there it was. But I did want to give a special attention to the Iranian members of that street, to people like Mahmoud Agha and his wife, because I was more certain of where their hearts went back to than I was sure of where anybody else's heart went back to. Even as much as I loved to hear Mahmoud Agha say So long, I couldn't get around the fact that So long was not in my blood. It was somewhere very close, and it was so close that sometimes that distance was negligible, both in writing and in life, but still it was not in the blood.

There was a while when it used to worry me that the American language used by the writers I loved did not come as naturally to me. I was the first person in my family to care about the sound of So long as much as I did. But there was something special about being the first one, too. You were the discoverer, and one day you woke up and discovered just how much *was* natural, because when I heard Mahmoud Agha say So long, I saw how much it touched something in me that was already there.

So, I started saying it myself, because how else was I supposed to get it into my blood other than by repeated use? And nobody batted an eye, just like they hadn't when Mahmoud Agha said it. It became natural pretty quickly, enough that I didn't have to think about it. It didn't make the effort of being an American writer any easier. I still had to sit down and find my own America before I could tell anybody what was happening there in the form of fiction. But the effort to find that America made the writing easier because I could be sure of where I was when I got there. It was an America where an Iranian storekeeper would say So long, even as his wife was telling me I was the American one for having been here so long, and it just reminded me again that everybody had something to say if you listened, and it evened out everything that was vast and unknowable about America to remember that I could always be a listener, I could always take in somebody else's America and grow my own by doing so, and know that I would have *something* to work with after doing that because at the very least, my America was a growing America.

If it hadn't been a countryman who was saying So long, if it had been somebody from anywhere else, I might've let the whole thing stay a mystery, but it became even more important to me to find out after I started saying So long, because it was an Iranian connecting me to an American past.

I knew there were Iranians who thought, why try to connect to an American past? But I didn't *not* want to connect to an Iranian past. That was why I went to Mahmoud's store in the first place. I wanted to connect to both. The reason was, I was interested in everything that's ever happened.

So, I was determined to find the root of it. I forgot my original theory that somebody was messing with Mahmoud Agha because it sounded too beautiful coming from his mouth to have an unpleasant source like that.

I still figured it was best to take an indirect approach. One day when his wife was behind the counter again, I asked her if she and Mahmoud Agha had learned English when they were still in Iran.

"No," she said. "We learned after we came here. We learned from movies."

"What kind of movies?"

"All kinds of movies. Except the shooting movies. They don't talk very much in them."

"What were the best movies to learn from?"

"All movies can teach something. But Mahmoud likes old movies. Black-and-white."

"He does?"

"Yes. He was working here when we first started, and he was learning the rules for selling alcohol. And he found out that there was a time in America when alcohol was illegal. Did you know this?"

"Yes."

"So, he came home and told me and we laughed because we said, 'it is just like Iran.' We were happy to discover this. I mean that it is a bad law, but we were happy to find out that they used to have this law in America, too. We thought, okay, it is like Iran here, now we understand. So, after that Mahmoud wanted to find out about this time for America, he became very interested. He wanted to watch all their old movies. Now I think maybe he has seen all of them. But he still finds some new ones.

"You know," she said. "It's nice to think that if they used to have this law in America but now they don't any more, maybe in Iran it will be gone someday, too."

"Yes," I said. "It is nice to think that."

"Of course, people in Iran still make alcohol. My cousin made wine in his house. It was very good."

"So I've heard," I said.

It was nice to walk home and think about Mahmoud Agha watching old black-and-white movies and learning English from them and learning other things, too. It was so nice that I felt small and foolish for needing to hear him say So long before asking about their lives. I should be wanting to hear about it before they even say a word, I thought. Their stories are bigger than one thing they happen to say.

Still, I was glad to have gotten to the bottom of it. After that, the biggest thrill for me of walking into Mahmoud Agha and his wife's store was when there was even just one American in there, because I knew that just after I picked up a pack of gum or a newspaper and went to the counter to pay for it, that American would hear two Iranian men say So long to each other, and by rights they would have to wonder what a big world it must be for a thing like that to occur.

NOBODY DIED

His memory was going, and old Ali Abhari had forgotten his e-mail password. Nothing he tried worked. He asked his wife.

"I wrote it down for you on a piece of paper," she said.

"Yes. And that was a very good idea. However, I cannot remember where I put that piece of paper."

"What do you remember about it?"

"It was one of the men I knew in prison. They killed him."

"Rouzbeh?"

"No."

"Karimi?"

"No."

"Haghighi?"

"No. They didn't kill him. They tortured him. They broke him though. Poor guy."

"Well," his wife said. "Kamran set up the account for you. You should ask him."

"Alright."

He went outside. His son had come to their house to mow the lawn.

Had those men really been killed? he thought. Yes. Was he still alive? Yes. Did the sun feel warm on his face? It did.

"Wasn't it Rouzbeh?" his son said.

"No. He was a great man, but it wasn't him."

"Well, who else was there?"

"There were many of them. Do you know how many of us there were? Enough to start a real country. It would have been a beautiful country now if they had all lived."

His son turned off the mower. It was wrong to have it going during this conversation.

"That is why I can't remember. There were so many. They killed them all."

His son didn't say anything for a little while.

"Well, was there anybody you were closest to?"

"There was Rouzbeh. There was Karimi. There was the man who taught me how to play chess."

"What was his name?"

"That is a good question."

His wife yelled from an open window.

"Was it Zifounoun?"

"Zifounoun? He didn't care about chess. He was an athlete."

"Who said anything about chess?"

"There was a man who taught me how to play chess."

"Well, if you can't remember his name, that's probably not it," his wife said.

"Good point. Is it possible I once knew his name?"

"It is possible," his son said.

Across the street from their house, their neighbor, a cheerful white man, came out to water his flowers. He waved, and Ali and his son waved back. The man did not know that the names they were trying to remember were those of men who were killed by men trained by America. It *almost* felt like America did not know. But in some secret parts of themselves, both America and the man knew.

Ali Abhari's son leaned against the lawnmower and tried to see the part of the man that knew the men his father was trying to remember had been killed by men trained by America.

"Hi," the man called out. "Nice day!"

"Yes," Ali said. "Beautiful!"

Well, his son thought, that wasn't it.

"Hmm," Ali said. "Perhaps it is one of the other men who lived."

"I didn't think there were many who lived," his son said.

"There were a few," Ali said. "But I don't think I would have chosen one of the ones who lived."

His son smiled. "You like the dead."

"I like *those* dead. I love them. The dead are very alive to me."

"What was it like when *they* were alive?"

"In prison? It was wonderful." Ali Abhari lit up in a way that made his son think that perhaps he would never die.

"I'm glad there was one place like that," his son said.

"Yes," Ali said. "But what was the man's name that is my password? I am ashamed that I cannot remember."

"It's alright. Those guys didn't know what e-mail was."

They laughed. The man across the street looked at them and thought they were very nice, the Iranians who lived across the street.

"You know," his son said. "There is a thing you can click and if you answer a question correctly, they will let you set up a new password."

Ali looked sad. "Yes, that is the thing I may have to do," he said. "But what if I don't know the answer to the question?"

"You chose the question yourself."

"I did?"

"Yes."

"How good of me," Ali said. "It seems that I must have

remembered that I can't remember anything."

"You just have to answer it and you can make a new password. Pick another one of the men."

Ali Abhari smiled. "How many must have died if there were men among them I can't even remember? Can you imagine? They gave us a cyanide capsule before we went in, in case the pain got too bad. I remember it all clearly. It is just the names."

His son looked at him. "Maybe you can still remember. Was it one of your teachers?"

"No," Ali said.

"Was it one of the Azerbaijanis?"

"No. There was only me and Tarrasoli," he said. "It is bad to not remember a man who died."

"You don't not remember *them*. You just don't remember the names."

Ali Abhari wanted to say that it was the same thing. But he knew his son was trying to make him feel better.

His wife leaned her head out the window.

"Did you capitalize it?" she called.

"What?"

"Did you capitalize the first letter in the name? Remember you forgot before."

"Capitalize," Ali said.

"It won't work if you were supposed to capitalize it," his son said.

They went inside. Ali's wife joined them at the computer. They all wanted to see.

Ali tried the first name, Rouzbeh, with a capital letter. It went straight to his e-mail.

They all cried out in joy. Ali Abhari was a young man again, because he remembered all the men he had known and loved in prison. Nobody died whom he couldn't remember. Nobody died and the revolution lived.

ACKNOWLEDGMENTS

The listed stories originally appeared in the following periodicals:

The Chattahoochee Review: "The Vine"

Chicago Quarterly Review: "Nobody Died"

COG: "The Outdoor Movie"

Columbia Journal: "You Are my Brother"

Glimmer Train: "The Tune"

Gulf Coast: "The Trophy"

Heavy Feather Review: "Joe West's Brother"

Hobart: "Fame"

The Hong Kong Review: "Fourteen"

JuxtaProse: "Young and Old"

Lost Coast Review: "So Long"

The Mighty Line: "All Is Lost"

Prime Number Magazine: "The Home Thing"

The Rumpus / California Prose Directory: "Sharpness"

Slippery Elm: "Argentina Versus France"

Sparkle & Blink: "The Overpayment" and "The Speaker's Apprentice"

Thumbnail Magazine: "The Myth"

The Turnip Truck(s): "Proverbs"

Washington Square: "Bee on a String"

West Branch Wired: "The Use of Language"

West Texas Literary Review: "The Wedding Speech"

Wigleaf: "The Calendar"

Your Impossible Voice: "Worth it To Be Wrong"

PREVIOUS WINNERS OF THE ORISON FICTION PRIZE

2018

Oceanography, stories by Jeremy Griffin
Selected by Lan Samantha Chang

2017

You or a Loved One, stories by Gabriel Houck
Selected by David Haynes

2016

Miss Portland, a novel by David Ebenbach
Selected by Peter Orner

ABOUT THE AUTHOR

Siamak Vossoughi was born in Tehran, Iran and currently lives in Seattle. His first story collection, *Better Than War*, received the 2014 Flannery O'Connor Award for Short Fiction. His stories have appeared in *Glimmer Train, Kenyon Review, The Missouri Review,* and *The Rumpus,* among other places.

ABOUT ORISON BOOKS

Orison Books is a 501(c)3 non-profit literary press focused on the life of the spirit from a broad and inclusive range of perspectives. We seek to publish books of exceptional poetry, fiction, and non-fiction from perspectives spanning the spectrum of spiritual and religious thought, ethnicity, gender identity, and sexual orientation.

As a non-profit literary press, Orison Books depends on the support of donors. To find out more about our mission and our books, or to make a donation, please visit www.orisonbooks.com.

For information about supporting upcoming Orison Books
titles, please visit www.orisonbooks.com/donate/, or write to
Luke Hankins at editor@orisonbooks.com.